This, My Second Life

PATRICK CHARNLEY

HUTCHINSON HEINEMANN

UK | USA | Canada | Ireland | Australia
India | New Zealand | South Africa

Hutchinson Heinemann is part of the Penguin Random House group of companies whose addresses can be found at global.penguinrandomhouse.com

Penguin Random House UK,
One Embassy Gardens, 8 Viaduct Gardens, London SW11 7BW

penguin.co.uk

First published 2026

001

Copyright © Patrick Charnley, 2026

The moral right of the author has been asserted

Penguin Random House values and supports copyright. Copyright fuels creativity, encourages diverse voices, promotes freedom of expression and supports a vibrant culture. Thank you for purchasing an authorised edition of this book and for respecting intellectual property laws by not reproducing, scanning or distributing any part of it by any means without permission. You are supporting authors and enabling Penguin Random House to continue to publish books for everyone. No part of this book may be used or reproduced in any manner for the purpose of training artificial intelligence technologies or systems. In accordance with Article 4(3) of the DSM Directive 2019/790, Penguin Random House expressly reserves this work from the text and data mining exception.

Set in 12.7/15.2pt Fournier MT Pro
Typeset by Six Red Marbles UK, Thetford, Norfolk

Printed and bound in Great Britain by Clays Ltd, Elcograf S.p.A.

The authorised representative in the EEA is Penguin Random House Ireland,
Morrison Chambers, 32 Nassau Street, Dublin D02 YH68

A CIP catalogue record for this book is available from the British Library

ISBN: 978–1–529–15525–9

Penguin Random House is committed to a sustainable future for our business, our readers and our planet. This book is made from Forest Stewardship Council® certified paper.

For Alexa

Author's Note

Before the opening of this novel, Jago Trevarno has a cardiac arrest and sustains a brain injury. Everything about those things in this novel is a true representation of my own experience. Other than that, this is a work of fiction.

I

It's dark outside my window, but only just. There's a faint pink light in the sky where the dawn is creeping over the horizon. I never draw my curtains because I like to see what's happening in the sky from my bed. It's darker than anything I've known at night here. Although, when the moon is bright, the light that comes into my room is almost like daylight and long shadows stretch across the floorboards. My room is in the attic so it's almost part of the sky.

Sometimes I wake up in the night having hallucinations. They're not nice, but Jacob hears me if I get out of bed and he comes in and sits in the chair in the corner until I fall back to sleep. It's been happening since I woke up from the coma, although I don't remember much of that time.

I can hear Jacob now, downstairs in the kitchen. This is my favourite time of day. It's almost completely silent apart from the soft clink of pans and crockery as Jacob moves around the kitchen getting the breakfast things ready. I've never seen Jacob rush anything. He moves slowly, deliberately, which suits me because I do things slowly too now. If he was rushing around I think it would make me feel that I've slowed down, and also I don't like fast movements. I can't keep up with what's going on.

I don't really remember how it was that I ended up

coming here, but Jacob says, with me not having any parents any more, the hospital called him. He visited me every week in hospital, even though it's a long way from here to Bristol. And he told me – over and over so that I'd remember – that I mustn't even think about what happens next. I was coming home with him and that was all I needed to know. On the day I was discharged, he went to my little studio flat in Bristol, picked up some of my things, and brought me down to Cornwall, and I've been here ever since.

Jacob will be down in the kitchen in his blue and green tartan dressing gown, and his slippers with the soles that are coming off so that they slap on the soles of his feet when he walks, like a seal's flippers. It's the same breakfast every day: bacon and eggs with toast. The bacon is thick-cut bacon that's juicy and salty. Jacob gets it from Rowan Tree Farm about half a mile down the track. He gets the eggs from there too, but never milk because we have cows. Sometimes he gets a chicken from the farm. That will last us three days. We have roast breast the first day, then a sort of casserole thing with beans in it the second day and chicken soup the third day. But a lot of the time we have beef from the herd.

Orange light from the oil lamps in the kitchen is coming up the stairs and through the crack where my door is slightly ajar. We use oil lamps and candles because there's no electricity in the farmhouse, apart from in the outside store where there's a deep freezer for the beef after slaughter. There could be electricity inside too, of course, but Jacob doesn't want it. He told me the neighbours think he's eccentric. I told him I think that's a compliment and he laughed. The lamps cast a soft light that doesn't quite fill the rooms so that at night it's dim in the corners. I'll get up when Jacob calls me, but for now I'll stay under the heavy blankets. I left my window open last night, and my room is chilly, so I'm delaying the moment of pulling back the covers.

I have a candle by my bed which I read by a little bit if I'm not too tired but I can't read much any more, just a couple of pages. Jacob gave me a little bible, even though I wouldn't say he's religious. It has a red cover and paper that's wafer thin. It's small enough to slip into a trouser pocket. Inside it says *Gideons*. They came to my school when I was eleven or twelve, the Gideons, and gave everyone a copy of the Bible, just like this one. At break time, after the Gideon people had left, some of the other boys made a big show of ripping up their bibles and throwing them up into the sky like confetti. I hung on to mine. It felt very special and sometimes I would read little bits in bed before I went to sleep. I promised God that I would read a bit every day and in the end I read all of Luke's Gospel because I liked the name. I wanted to change my name to Luke for a while, not because of the Bible but because there was a boy down the road called Luke who was good at everything and was nice too, which isn't always the case in my experience.

I believed in God back then. I'm not sure I do now. I liked going to church with my mother when I was little, sitting close to her on the cool wooden pew. I especially liked the roof of the church. I would gaze up at it and think about the geometry of the oak beams that looked like a giant net. When my mum asked me what I was looking at and I told her, she said maybe I could be an engineer. I would think about that a lot when I was making things with my wooden bricks at home, but I didn't say anything because it felt like something that might happen to someone else, not me.

The other thing I liked was the smells in the church. There was the ordinary church smell, which smelled of cool still air that wasn't exactly stale but not fresh either. And then at special masses there was the smell of incense which the priest burnt in a crucible thing that he would waft over people's heads. It smelled sweet and foreign and exotic.

The best thing of all about church, though, was confession. As a child at least. You went into the church and joined the sort of scattered queue that formed in the pews nearest to the confessional box. That's the little room where the priest sat waiting for people. For sinners.

You'd go in and say, 'Forgive me, Father, for I have sinned.' Then you'd list out your sins from the past week, or some of them anyway, the ones you chose to share. After you'd done that, the priest would give you a penance, which is the Catholic way of saying punishment, then he would absolve you of your sins until the next week when you'd do it all again.

As a child, I used confession to see off a telling-off by my mum for the bad things I had done. Well, naughty really, not actually bad. This is why confession was the best bit about church.

For example, one birthday a friend gave me a battery-powered helicopter with blades that spun around with lights. I was so sure it would fly if I could just throw it out of the window at the top of the cottage and it would soar around the rooftops. But it was just a toy, and my mum made me promise not to. I really wanted it to fly, though, so much that I really did believe it might if I could just give it the chance. So one day, when Mum was out, I launched it out of my bedroom window. I watched as it climbed briefly into the air from the power of my throw, but then it dropped. It crashed in the courtyard below and smashed into lots of pieces. I was really upset about it, but mostly I was afraid of what my mum would do. And she was going be really angry, not so much because I had broken that helicopter, but because I had promised her I wouldn't do what I had done. Also, we didn't have a lot of money, and Mum always told me we must look after the things we had.

So, I hid the wreckage of the helicopter in the bottom of my wardrobe, and that Saturday, at confession, I confessed what I had done to the priest. I did my ten Hail Marys as my penance and I was forgiven. By God at least.

I told Mum on the walk home. It was a tricky one for her. God had forgiven me as she always said he would if I confessed my sins, but I had broken the helicopter and tricked her on top of it. At first I thought she was going to be really cross, but then she put her arm around me and laughed and said, 'I can see I am going to have to watch you.'

So, although we went to mass and confession, it wasn't like Mum went in for the Ten Commandments and sin and all that in a big way. She wasn't a literal person. She believed in God, Jesus and Mary – especially Mary – but she wasn't one for the rules of the Church or anywhere else for that matter. It seemed to me that being Catholic was more of a feeling for her. Not like those people at church trying to show how holy they were, holding out their hands to receive the Lord like

He was coming down on them right there and then, and we'd all better watch to see just how holy they were and, more importantly, how much holier they were than everyone else. And there were a few of those people. Sometimes it was just the expression on their faces – a sort of put-on holiness – that would make me and my mum give each other a secret look, and then we'd laugh about it on the way home. She said it wasn't very Catholic to be so showy.

When I think about it, it was a bit odd that she was a Catholic because she chose to be one; she wasn't baptised as a baby, or even as a child. She already had me when she was baptised. And the reason it was odd, I thought, was because she was also a feminist, plus she'd had me without being married. But I suppose everyone is the sum of their contradictions.

Mum died just before I turned nineteen and I'm twenty now. It was cancer, of course, and a really fast one. It was only a few months after she was diagnosed that she died. Even though she was young – only forty-six – I don't think she was scared of dying. She was more worried about me. *There'll be some money from the house, and you've got Jacob and Sophie.* Sophie was my girlfriend. Mum kept saying that over and over and I know she did it to try to reassure herself as much as anything. She didn't want to think she was leaving me on my own.

The night she died she had the priest over and after he had gone I asked her what he had said. She had her eyes closed and she didn't say anything.

Later when I was sitting with her, she came round for a

short time, and she looked at me and said, 'There are flowers where I'm going.'

'You mean after you die?' I asked, and she just smiled and closed her eyes again. That's why I don't think dying scared her.

When she died later that night, there was a strong gust of wind and the window in her bedroom slammed with a bang and the candle on the windowsill blew out. I'll never forget that.

Although, when I came out of the coma, I wasn't sure whether she was dead or alive. I had a feeling she might have died, but I couldn't remember. I asked one of the nurses why my mum hadn't come to visit and she held my hand and told me she had died. I wasn't sad. Actually I didn't feel anything at all. It was as if the brain injury had turned off all my emotions like a switch in my head. It was just a fact, nothing more.

I don't remember my father at all, but that's not because of the brain injury. I never knew him. He left my mum when she was pregnant. Jacob's the closest I have to a father. He's my mum's older brother, but he's never tried to be a dad to me. He's just Jacob.

As I said, I don't think Jacob's religious, in spite of his name and giving me that bible. He doesn't go to church, or have little crosses and icons or anything like the ones we had on the walls at home when I was young. There is a church here, though, just over the fields, not far away. A chapel, really. I go into it if I happen to be passing on one of my walks. I've never seen anyone else there. It has thick granite walls and a squat doorway that you have to stoop through to go inside. Well, I do because I'm almost six feet tall. It's dark and cool and very peaceful inside with the same smell of very old beeswaxed wood that I remember from the church at home in St Ives.

I don't pray. As I said, I'm not sure I even believe in God. After I had the cardiac arrest and got the brain injury I thought there couldn't be a God. Not because I thought no God would let something like that happen, but because I didn't see God or anything else when my heart stopped and I stopped breathing. No tunnel of white light, no light at all, no floating above myself. Nothing. My heart wasn't beating and I wasn't breathing. Clinically I was dead, and for a long time; forty minutes it took them to get my heart going again. Surely if there was a God I would have seen something, even if it was the Devil? So, for a little while I thought that was proof there is no God and no heaven. You die and that's it. But then I talked to Granny Carne about it and she said it wasn't proof of anything. She said that because people were trying to resuscitate me, I hadn't crossed over yet. I thought that also made sense, so I haven't made my mind up about all of that.

Granny Carne's not actually my granny. She's not even Jacob's granny, which would make her my great-granny if she was, but that's what we call her. She lives up the hill from here. Her cottage is set back in a crease in the land so that it can't be seen unless you're almost at the door. Her garden slopes steeply up the hill behind the cottage and from the top of the garden you can see all the way down to the sea and everything in between. So, she's hidden away, but she can still see everything around her like an eagle in its nest.

She has second sight, too. The first time I saw her after the cardiac arrest she took my hands in hers. They were strong and chestnut-brown from the sun. She said, 'What's happened to you has changed you. You'll be glad of it in time.'

I didn't take it in at the time. It does take me longer to understand things now. I hear what's being said, but I don't process it straight away. They called it a processing-speed impairment in the rehab hospital. At dinner that evening I asked Jacob what he had told Granny Carne about what had happened to me.

'Nothing,' he said. 'Only that you were staying with me for a while. I thought I'd leave it to you to say whatever you want to say about it.'

Then I told him what Granny Carne had said to me.

'Well, she does have second sight,' he said.

'You mean she's psychic?'

'She feels things, you know that.'

She could have been guessing, or putting two and two together, or just heard about in the way that news travels on the breeze in these parts, I thought. It's obvious that something had happened to me. It didn't feel like that, though. It seemed like she knew all about it and that she really cared. Although I have known her all my life really, so she would care. I was born in St Ives and that's where me and Mum lived until she died, and we were always coming over here to visit Jacob as he was her brother. It's only twenty minutes down the coast from St Ives to here if you're driving. Jacob would visit us too, but I liked coming here and seeing the cows and riding the horses. I can't even remember when I started riding, I was that young. And we'd often see Granny Carne. We'd drop in for tea, or just bump into her in the lanes.

Anyway, I started to spend more time with Granny Carne after seeing her that first time after the cardiac arrest. On my walks I would find myself coming towards her cottage without really planning to go there. And she would always seem to be expecting me when I came. I like going there and sitting and chatting with her. She and Jacob are my only relations now, even though I'm not really related to Granny Carne.

I'll get up now. I can smell bacon and coffee and I'm hungry. I pull my dressing gown from the bed post and put on my watch. Jacob said there's no need for me to be awake at the same time as him and usually I'm not, but the sun is up so early at the moment and sometimes I can't sleep through it. I go to bed early and I sleep in the afternoons, and that means I get enough rest. They say sleep is the best thing for brain injury and I need to sleep a lot more than I used to. Eleven or twelve hours plus rests and sleeps in the day. This is early for me to get up but as I'm awake, I may as well.

I swing my legs out of bed. The floorboards are cool beneath my feet. Even on very hot days this house doesn't get very warm. It's the walls, thick granite with small square windows and flagstones on the ground floor, which feel so good under my bare feet when it's hot outside. Jacob says the house is over two hundred years old.

'Morning,' he says as I come down the stairs.
'Morning.'
'Sleep well?'

'Pretty well.'

'Good. There's coffee in the pot.'

'How about you? Did you sleep all right?'

'Oh yes,' he says as he always does. 'I'm going to make a start on the fence in the bottom field today if you want to help after you've done the milking,' he adds.

'OK.'

'Only if you want to, though.'

'I do want to.' I like doing stuff with Jacob. He's careful, though. He doesn't want to overload me or make me feel like I have to do things.

It was me who asked him if I could milk the cows. He thought it would be better if I stayed in bed for longer, but I like doing it, and it's not as if the cows need to be milked at dawn, so long as I don't leave it too late or they'll be uncomfortable or even get mastitis, which can be really dangerous.

Jacob has a small herd of Devon Red Ruby cattle. They're huge beasts, rusty-coloured with handlebar horns just like the sort you would see on a ranch in a Western. There are nine bullocks, one bull and two cows. The bull keeps the cows in milk by getting them pregnant once a year. Then each year there are two calves to be sold at market if they're heifers or raised for beef if they're bullocks. The nine bullocks come from a farm near the Lizard and Jacob buys them as young calves and raises them until they are ready for slaughter, then does it all over again. It's a good system for Jacob as he has plenty of land for pasture but wouldn't be able to manage a full herd and all the breeding on his own. He also keeps a lot of beef for us out in the deep freezer.

He calls the two cows 'the ladies': Anna and Agnetha,

named after the singers in ABBA, which made me laugh when he first told me. Their milk is thick and creamy, nothing like the milk you get from the shop, and the butter we make from the milk is almost luminous, like buttercups. We make it in a churn the old-fashioned way, pounding it up and down like a piston. This is how Jacob does everything on the farm, in the way things used to be done. That's why he doesn't bother with electricity – he doesn't see the need for it. It's a small farm, just the cattle and the things he grows for the farmers' market. I shouldn't think Jacob makes a great deal of money from it, but he doesn't want more than he needs.

I spread butter thickly on my toast and take a big bite. The bread is homemade and dense and the melted butter oozes back out of it as I chew. I'm always hungry these days. I crave carbs and fat and sugar. Jacob likes heavy food, or hearty food as he calls it, so that's another good thing about living here with him. He's not so much into the sweet things as I am nowadays, though. I buy bags and bags of sweets from Mrs Beaton who runs the village shop. She says the dentist will have to start paying her commission. She has some posh chocolate, the sort with lots of cocoa and flavours like chilli and sea salt, made by a woman in Hayle. 'The visitors like that sort of thing,' she said when she saw me pick up a bar and put it back down. She meant the holidaymakers. Some people call them emmets, but that's a bit rude, really. There aren't so many around here, but they pass through our little hamlet on their way to Zennor or St Just.

I prefer cheap chocolate: Milky Bar buttons, Dairy Milk and Maltesers mainly; as well as sweets, especially the chewy ones. In the evenings after we've cleared up the dinner things and checked on the animals, I get into the chocolates and sweets. I suppose it's not good for me, but I'm not bothered. One evening, not long after I came here, Jacob said, smiling, 'You like your sweet things, don't you?' and that was all he had to say about it. He's not one to comment on other people's ways, or to mind what they do, as long as they're not hurting anybody else. I told one of my neurologists about it and she said the brain needs a lot of energy to repair, so I think it must be OK.

I pour myself some coffee, which is the other thing I like to have a lot of. The sun is up now, and a shaft of light from the window over the kitchen sink cuts across the heavy oak table, picking out all of the scars and dimples in the wood. Like everything in this house, the table is ancient and feels like it belongs here.

'So how do we fix the fence?' I ask.

'Well, to begin with, we'll set the posts. There's quite a lot of digging at first, I'll do that, then it's a case of setting the posts in the ground and nailing on the planks. I'll do the heavy stuff and you can help with the rest. If it's not too much, like.'

'It won't be,' I say. I lost a lot of weight in hospital. It just falls off you even though you're lying there. They say being in a coma is like running a marathon each day. I suppose that's why I'm so hungry now.

Jacob comes over with the frying pan and piles bacon and eggs on to my plate. We eat in silence. Neither of us much likes noise in the mornings. Once we've finished, I take the dishes and wash them up. I use water from the big black kettle on the stove. Jacob only lights the water boiler at the end of every other day so we can each have a bath in the evening before dinner, and also on laundry day which is Saturday. It's a big copper boiler in the corner of the kitchen, sitting on top of a wood burner that heats the water. It takes quite a while to warm up but not as long as you might think.

Everything is slower here. That's how we live. It's also how I need to live now. After my mum died I was restless and I couldn't settle, always doing something, keeping busy. I was fit and healthy, or I thought I was anyway. In St Ives, before the cardiac arrest, I worked in the café on Porthmeor, did odd jobs here and there and gave surf lessons in the season. When I wasn't working I surfed and ran, and went for long walks. I never just did nothing. I knew I had heart disease, but it was just a fact that was given to me by a cardiologist who saw me after the GP heard a heart murmur one time when I had a chest infection. I just tossed it to the side. Something to think about later. And my mum was dead by then so she wasn't around to worry about it, and I didn't even bother telling Jacob. And then me and Sophie broke up and I moved to Bristol and I tried to put St Ives, my mum, Sophie and everything else out of my mind.

It did get worse, though, my heart, and the doctors in Bristol said I would need surgery to fix a leaking valve, only I don't remember being told that because days later my heart stopped and my memories of that, and many more, were erased from my mind. The only reason I know it is that I still have the letter from the doctor. When I came across it in my things that Jacob got from my flat in Bristol, it was like finding a piece of a puzzle.

After I've washed up, I go back to my room, put on my

clothes and brush my teeth in the little sink in the corner of the room. It's fully light now outside. I look at my reflection in the small mirror on the wall. I look better now I've been here for a while. My skin is brown instead of the dishwater white that it was before, and my cheeks are less hollow. I'm still thin and I need to get my strength back but I'm improving with the work on the farm and eating Jacob's meals.

'Are you coming?' Jacob calls up the stairs.

'Just a minute,' I shout down through a mouthful of toothpaste, speckling the mirror with white spots.

2

Out in the yard Jacob is checking the straps that are holding the fence posts and wooden slats on to the back of the cart. It's a beautiful cart, a box cart Jacob told me, which just means it's like an open box on wheels. The back wheels reach almost to my shoulder and their wooden spokes are painted a proud navy blue, the same as the sides of the cart itself. Like everything Jacob owns, it's really well looked after.

'Will you fetch Niamh?' Jacob asks. 'It's not good for her to be pulling heavy loads what with being in foal, but this is very light and she'll welcome a bit of exercise.'

I say I will, and I go over to the stable, which is part of the house really. The barn where the cattle sleep is next to that. I like thinking of us and the horses and the cows all close together at night.

Niamh is enormous. She's a carthorse and she's taller than me by quite a bit. Jacob says she weighs almost a tonne. She's beautiful, glossy black apart from her white socks and a white diamond on her nose. Her eyes are very dark and they shine like onyx. She likes to work and has an eagerness when she stoops to put her head through the harness.

The other horse is Connor, a chestnut-brown Welsh cob. He's the one I ride. You can ride along the lanes around here as there's hardly any cars even in high season because it's mostly just farms. The best thing to do, though, is to take him over the fields. No one grows crops here. It's all rough pasture so people don't mind if you ride over their land. Well, almost no one. Bill Sligo up at Blackheath Farm doesn't want anyone on his land. There's a couple of public footpaths over his farm and he lets the brambles grow over the gaps in hedges on to his fields. He's not supposed to do that, but because we're out of the way, no one bothers to say anything. Most of the walkers stick to the coastal path, not the fields, anyway. He likes to walk over Jacob's land, though, Bill Sligo. Sometimes I see him from my window, going down the lane to Jacob's bottom field and the coastal path. I can tell it's him from a distance, even with my eyesight, as he swaggers along.

That's where we are working today, down by the cliffs. Part of the fence on the boundary with the coastal path has come down. It's dangerous because the cattle could get out and walk off the cliff edge. They're not the cleverest of animals. Jacob's got them in one of the top fields for the time being but they need to be rotated around the fields so the grass can grow back after they've grazed. I still can't get over how all they eat is grass but from that they make so much milk and meat.

I put on my boots and go along to the stable. Niamh and Connor already have their heads out of the stable door. We only close it at night if the weather's bad and it's been really good lately, sunny and warm, and it's good again today. The sky is a sharp deep blue that I feel I could dive into when I look up at it. The sun bounces off the horses' heads and makes them shine like conkers.

'Hello,' I say, walking towards them. They both push their noses at me, urging me to smooth them. I put a hand on to each of their noses and they push gently against me and shuffle their hooves in the hay. They know we're going out. I'll take Connor with us so he can be out in the field while we work. I take him whenever I go out really, if I can. It's much nicer than driving around would be, although I can't drive anyway because of the trouble I have with my vision from the brain injury and because my thinking is too slow. The impairments, as doctors call them.

I don't like much the word 'impaired'. A while ago I looked it up to see where it came from. All I remember is something about Canadians using it to describe drink-driving a long time ago, and it made me dislike the word a bit less because having a brain injury does feel a bit like you've drunk too much, or it does to me anyway. Not really drunk, but the feeling after a couple of pints when you feel sort of cocooned and a bit separate from everything else. I'm also quite wobbly when I walk.

Niamh's harness is a big oval hoop, the sort of thing you see hanging on the wall of a country pub. I lift it off the tack wall and bring it out to the courtyard, encouraging the horses to follow me. Niamh dips her head so that I can slip it over. I don't saddle Connor as he won't want it on while we're working. I just slip on his bridle so that I can ride him bareback down the track.

I put my foot on the cart's wheel and jump up on to him. He makes a supple movement with his back as I settle on him. We were made for each other, me and Connor. Our bodies fit together perfectly and when we ride, we move like the pistons of an engine.

'We'll see you down there,' Jacob says with a laugh. He knows I want to have a gallop before we start on the fence. Connor needs it too. He'll be restless if he hasn't got rid of some energy before I settle him in the field.

'Come on,' I say, giving him a gentle tap with my heel. We come out of the yard and down the lane that leads to the bottom field. There's dew on the hedgerows, which rise high on either side of the lane. It makes the yellow flowers of the gorse sparkle. They smell of coconut and the summer.

In a few minutes we're at the bottom of the lane, round the last corner, and there's the sea.

'Let's go,' I call to Connor and squeeze his flank. He shoots forwards like a coiled spring let go. The dewy grass swooshes around Connor's hooves. I fix my eyes on the horizon and it's like we're riding over the water and out to sea.

We're racing down towards the cliff and Connor's back is rippling like a fish. There's no sound apart from our breathing and the thudding of Connor's hooves in the soft earth. We're getting closer to the bottom of the field now, to the gap in the bracken that opens to the cliff path and the sea beyond, but I don't see it. My eyes are on the perfect line between the sea and the sky. My heart is pounding now with the thrill of it, but my breath is deep and calm. I lean into Connor, urging him on, but he senses the danger as we near the cliff edge. He rears up and comes back down to the earth with a thud and stands solidly still like a statue, both of us breathing hard.

'Good boy,' I whisper. 'You're my seahorse, aren't you?'

We stand there without moving, watching the sea. A single fishing boat chugs up the coast towards St Ives, close to the cliffs, and much further out a tanker grinds its way along the horizon.

I've always liked the idea of being on a tanker. I like all boats, really. It's the self-sufficiency of them, taking everything on board that you might need and stowing it away. And the feeling of being tucked up in a cabin at night with the engine vibrating below you and the ship heaving slowly from side to side. Even in storms I like it. Especially in storms. I've never felt at risk on a boat or a ship, unlike on planes where anything could happen.

Connor sidesteps a foot or so as a signal that he wants to get going.

'All right,' I say, nudging his flank with my boot, 'come on then.' We turn around and trot back up the field, passing Jacob and Niamh on their way down with the loaded cart.

'I'll just put Connor in the top field and I'll be down,' I call to him.

'Right you are.'

In the top field I unbuckle Connor's reins and walk back down towards the gap in the broken fence where Jacob is. Connor can still see us from the top field, which he likes, I think.

When I get back down, Jacob's already unloaded half the posts and he's laying them out where they will go. The broken part of the fence is only a few metres wide – three or four – but we are going to replace more of the posts because they're rotting, Jacob says.

First we pull out the old posts and load them on to the

cart. Then we start digging out the holes. Jacob has a special tool that scoops out the earth like a giant pair of pliers. I don't do much, but by mid-morning my shirt is still wet with sweat. When we stop for a drink I peel it off and lay it on the grass, which is now completely dry as if there hadn't been a dew at all. The sun is now high in the sky and there are only a few puffs of white cloud. It's hot for this late in September.

'That scar's looking better, ain't it,' Jacob says, nodding towards my chest.

'Yeah,' I say, looking down at the fine line running along my sternum. I run my fingers over it absent-mindedly. It's three months since the surgery and I still have to be careful while the bone is healing, so I'm not doing the digging. I'll hold the posts so Jacob can smash them down into the ground with his sledgehammer.

Jacob is strong. He's tall and broad and his hands are about half the size of mine again. He's the sort of man you can't imagine ever dying. I'm not sure exactly how old he is. He was quite a bit older than my mum, his sister, I do know that. I tried to work out how old my mum would be if she was still alive, but I can't remember what year she was born. These details of my life are out of reach. When I try to remember them, my mind sort of fuzzes up like a sudden fog rolling off the sea and shrouding the land.

I look at Jacob unloading the rest of the fresh logs from the cart, his body moving with the strength and smooth motion of a machine, just like Connor.

'Can you manage these, do you think?' Jacob asks, nodding towards the slats for the fence that he has unloaded into a neat pile on the grass. 'One at a time like,' he adds. 'But only if it's not too much. Don't push yourself. Here, try this,' he says, passing one over to me.

'Yeah, that's fine,' I say, taking it from him. I'm sure he knew it would be all right because he'd never ask me to do anything I couldn't do. He's not the sort that thinks you should always be pushing yourself. Whenever we talk about my recovery from the surgery or the brain injury and how long things might take, he always says the same thing. *All in good time.* And the way he says it, so gentle and reassuring, I feel it must be true, even though I know that really it isn't. That really my brain will never just go back to how it was before, just as the scar on my chest will never completely fade. And sometimes I do wonder what's going to happen to me, what's going to happen next.

I still have the flat in Bristol. I bought it with what was left after the executors of Mum's will had paid off the mortgage on our cottage. She made a living for us cleaning holiday lets because she could work while I was at school and be home when I got back. After a while, she set up a little cleaning business with her best friend, Sheila, and she saved and saved to get a deposit for our cottage. It was a granite stone cottage with shutters on the windows and two bedrooms and a kitchen-living room when you came in, and we both loved it. She made the curtains by hand, with stripy yellow fabric, and covers for the sofa and armchair that we got from the Salvation Army, and we painted the walls sky blue. In the evenings we would bolt the door and fasten the shutters and it felt so safe and cosy.

Some people might think the money I got from the sale of the cottage wasn't much after the mortgage was paid off, but to me it was a great deal, and it felt like even more because I knew how hard my mum had worked to get it. Later, when I went to Bristol, I spent almost every penny of it on my studio flat on the eighth floor of a block of flats in the centre of town. It was just a room really, but I felt like Bristol was a great ship and I was perched way above it in the crow's nest, looking down on to the lights of the city, at the great cathedral in the centre that was lit up at night as if the sun was shining on it, and the docks and the hills to the south. I knew Mum would have been pleased that I had somewhere no one could kick me out of or take away from me.

Maybe I will go back to it – I don't know. When will decisions be made about my future, and who will make them? I don't know the answer to that, so in these moments, when uncertainty makes my stomach knot, I think of Jacob and I think to myself: *All in good time.*

'OK, well, you need to lay two of these on the ground between where I'm putting the posts, then once we've got the posts in, we'll nail the slats to them. We're doing all right, it's coming along already,' Jacob says, making my thoughts dissolve.

After another half an hour or so, Jacob goes to his bag and rummages through it.

'I thought I brought some of that cake we got from Mrs Beaton yesterday,' he says, 'but I've gone and left it on the side in the kitchen. How about you go up and get it? There's some bread and cheese in the pantry if you want to bring that down too, and that'll do us for lunch.'

Up at the house, I put the bread and cheese into a paper bag and cut two large slices of cake, wrapping them in greaseproof paper. I look around for a bag to carry it all back down to the field. I know Jacob has bags for shopping somewhere – I've seen them, I'm sure. But where?

I look around the kitchen, opening drawers, checking the back of the door. I spend so much of my time looking for things these days, partly because my memory is so bad, but also there's this thing with my vision. Simultanagnosia. I have to say it slowly, syllable by syllable, or I can't get it right. It's kind of like tunnel vision but not quite. It means I can only see the thing I am looking directly at, and not anything around it. So if I'm looking for something I have to look straight at it or I'll miss it.

'It must frustrate you,' someone said to me – I can't remember who. But it doesn't. Bother me, that is. It's just how it is now. I don't get frustrated much. The other problem is I now have hardly any visual memory, so although I'm sure I've seen a bag somewhere I can't even begin to visualise where that might have been, or when I might have seen it.

I give up looking and go upstairs to fetch my backpack. It's on the window seat, and I'm just about to turn to go back downstairs when, out of the window, I see movement in the lane heading down towards the bottom field. The top of someone's head is moving along the hedgerow, and then they disappear.

All I saw was their hair, but I'm sure it's Bill Sligo. He has thick wiry black hair, the sort that would never stay in place no matter how much you combed it. I wonder what he's doing. I don't like the way he walks over Jacob's land like he owns it. I must remember to tell Jacob that I saw him. I start repeating it to myself *saw Bill Sligo, saw Bill Sligo, saw Bill*

Sligo. If I say that to myself all the way back down to the field, I'll remember it. I go back downstairs, and head out of the door, walking towards the lane when I stop and think I should probably have had a glass of water. Then I remember the bottle of water that I put with the bread and cheese and the cake. I've left it all in the kitchen and I'm carrying an empty backpack. I go back, get the food and the water. Have I got everything? I run through it in my head, satisfied that I have. I pull the door behind me and head back down the lane, thinking about the posts and the slats and how I've taken longer than I meant to.

When I get down there, Jacob looks up from the hole he's digging.

'Everything all right?' he asks.

'Yeah, fine,' I say. 'Sorry, it took longer than I thought.'

'No bother,' he says, and he means it. Jacob won't say anything he doesn't mean.

'It's getting there.' He gestures along the row of fence posts that are now standing perfectly upright in the ground. 'Couple more and we'll be ready for the slats, but let's have something to eat first. You must be hungry.'

'You must be, more like,' I say, laughing. How long had I been? I look at my wrist but I forgot to put on my watch this morning.

Jacob tears off a piece of bread and leans against the cart.

'When did they close the mine?' I ask, looking towards the wall of the wheelhouse that stands solid in the bottom corner of the field.

'Not long before the First World War. And that was how my great-grandpa, your great-great-grandpa, bought that land, as you know. The mining company was selling off land cheap.'

'Do you think there's still tin down there?'

'More than likely. Copper too, perhaps. They closed the mines because it wasn't worth the candle. Getting whatever was left out, that is. And mind you don't get any ideas about goin' down there to look, neither. It's a death trap.'

'I know,' I said. He and my mum must have told me a thousand times not to go near it.

'It don't matter how old a boy is, he's always drawn to that mine.'

'I'm twenty.'

'Like I said, it doesn't matter what age you are. No, there's no saying what state that mine's in. Reckon it could cave in if someone said boo down there, if it hasn't already.'

'So why wasn't it sealed up when it was closed?'

'Usual reason. Money. And the war. They left it for whoever bought the land to deal with. It's the same all over these parts. There was an effort to make the mines on public land safe, but if it was privately owned you just had to deal with it yourself, which is a bit much when most of the land has public footpaths going over it, but there we are. When I was a boy and started to show an interest in it, my grandpa put a cover over it, locked it up, and threw away the key. And that's how it's been ever since.'

I take a bite of bread and cheese and think about this, imagining the mineshaft dropping down below the wheelhouse, and the cool musty air down there. Most of the mine would have flooded when the men stopped working it and pumping the water out constantly, but there would still be parts above sea level, maybe beneath this field even. Probably beneath this field. Jacob says the land round here's like honeycomb. It makes me wonder if the whole farm could just fold into the ground one day as if it had never been there.

'Bit of cake?' Jacob asks after we've had the bread and cheese.

'Oh, yes please,' I say, taking it from him and putting a chunk straight into my mouth. Lemon and sugar ooze from it as I chew.

'Come on then,' Jacob says as he brushes crumbs off his shirt front with both hands, 'just the slats to go and we'll be done with this.'

Doing the slats is quick work. I hold each one in place while Jacob nails them in. He hits the nails so true with the hammer that they sink into the timber with only a couple of strikes. While Jacob puts his tools on to the cart, I fetch Niamh and then go to the top field to get Connor. His gait is relaxed now after burning off the restless energy that fizzed through him like electricity this morning.

When we get back to the house, there's a brown paper package on the doorstep. I pick it up and can tell straight away what it is: a fish. I take it inside and unwrap it on the kitchen table. It's a sea bass, a big one. Its silver skin shimmers like a mermaid's tail.

'That'll be from Samuel,' Jacob says.

Samuel is a fisherman from St Ives. He takes his little boat out and he spears fishes when the sea is flat and glassy and he can spot the glint of scales beneath the surface. I like his boat. It's an old one, made of wood and painted a deep burgundy colour with brilliant white around the gunwales. It has an ancient outboard engine that coughs and splutters, but it keeps chugging on.

'You have a rest and I'll sort that fish out in a bit.'

I don't try to say I'll help. I'm drained from the work. Upstairs in my room, I lie on my bed and try to think about the labyrinth of mineshafts deep down below the bottom field, but in an instant I'm asleep.

3

I wake to the sound of Jacob calling 'dinner' up the stairs. I've been asleep for hours. The brilliant light of the day has given way to the beginnings of a dusty-pink sunset. I stretch out in my bed and feel a pleasant ache through my body from the work.

'That looks good,' I say when I come down the stairs into the kitchen to see the fish on the table. Jacob's baked it in a salt crust that sparkles in the evening sunlight streaming through the kitchen window. Jacob cracks it open with the blunt edge of the knife and fragrant steam billows out. There are new potatoes too, with chunky crystals of sea salt and melting butter. The greens are from the walled kitchen garden just outside the back door. We grow a lot out there for ourselves, in the kitchen garden, and a lot more for the farmers' market in the small field nearest the house that isn't for pasture for the cows.

The flesh slides off the bone as Jacob fillets the fish. It's light and a little sweet with a slight flavour of the rosemary sprigs that Jacob stuffed into its cavity. We don't talk during dinner. We're both hungry. I have two helpings of potatoes, then sit back in my chair and let out a big sigh.

'Happy?' Jacob asks, his weathered face creased into a warm smile.

'Very.'

A bit later, after I've finished the washing up and I've poured him a coffee, I tell Jacob I'm going for a walk.

I take a stick with me and swish it along the bottom of the hedgerow as I walk down the lane towards the fields and the coast path beyond. The sea glitters below the late-evening sun, which is now big and dirty orange. The summer is almost over, but there's still a lot of warmth in the sun.

As I get to the bottom of the field, there, to my right, is the wheelhouse, its thick granite walls glowing in the sunset like golden sand. It grows bigger and bigger as I walk towards it until I'm standing in the dense tufts of grass at the base of the sea-facing wall. I reach out to touch the stone. It's rough and warm. Above my head, brambles spill out of the gap where the doorway would once have been. I walk all around the perimeter, stopping in front of the empty doorway. It's not at ground level, but about four feet up from the grass. There must have been wooden steps or something when it was working.

I pull myself up with my hands on the ledge above me, my feet finding a good grip on the rough granite as I clamber up. I stand and look out to sea and down the cliff in front of me. Everything is exactly as it would have been one hundred years ago, one thousand years ago, more even. I think about the last miner to have left the mine as he walked out through this doorway. What would he have done, out in the world looking for work along with the other miners who must also have been laid off when the mine was closed? Worked on the land, I suppose, or maybe some went up to Truro, Exeter, or even further up country.

I look down to where the mineshaft would be, in the middle of the wheelhouse. The ground is mostly overgrown with brambles and grass, but I can just see a glimpse of wood beneath the undergrowth. I think I expected to see a big drop and a deep shaft after what Jacob had said about staying away, but there's no gaping hole. I look more carefully now and see wooden slats beneath the undergrowth. I lower myself down on to the edge of the grass and stamp my foot while still holding myself up on the wall in case the wood is rotten and it crumbles away, but the wooden slats seem very solid. Bending down, I take two thick bramble branches between my forefinger and thumb, being careful not to grasp the thorns. I expect them to be firmly rooted in place, but when I pull, they lift away easily. In the spot they were covering, the slats are clearly a trap door. I crouch there, holding up the brambles and looking at them. There is something about them that isn't right, but my brain won't process it. As I touch the smooth wood, I realise what it is. The wood is new. I trace the edge of it with my eyes and see something shiny on the far side. I go round to it and carefully pull aside the brambles in that spot. It's a padlock and a sliding bolt, the sort you might put on a shed or an outhouse. The bolt, too, is new.

But Jacob had said that his grandpa had locked the entrance to the shaft and that it had been the same ever since. It's obviously been replaced, and recently, too. If Jacob didn't do it, then who did? And why? I sit on the ledge watching the sun sinking into the sea, and wondering whether I should ask Jacob about it.

It's strange how the sun seems to speed up when it goes below the horizon. I can see it slipping away until there is just a shimmering sliver of brilliant burnt orange, then it's gone.

I won't say anything to Jacob. I don't want him to know that as soon as he told me not to go near the mine, I went straight down there. It's not like I've found something dangerous he needs to know about. If anything, it must be safer than it would have been before. Still, as I walk back in the falling light, I feel uneasy about what I've seen. Someone has come on to Jacob's farm and done something without asking him.

Jacob is sitting in his chair, reading, when I come into the kitchen. I don't linger because I don't want to lie to him.

'Nice walk?' he asks, looking up at me.

' I saw the sunset,' I say, and then carry on quickly in case he asks me anything else. 'I'm going to head up now.'

'Good idea,' he says. 'Sleep well.'

'Thanks, you too. 'Night.'

''Night then.' He smiles before looking back down at his book. I pause on the stairs, thinking maybe I should just tell him what I've seen, but I'm worried he'd think bad of me so I carry on up, brush my teeth and get into bed. I make my breath sound like the sea with a lazy swell. A deep breath in and the little waves on the beach are sucked down and away, the last of them fizzing into the sand, then I breathe out slowly as the wave collapses back on to the beach.

4

Next day, I wake up at first light. I'm tired and need to sleep more, but I'm thinking about the mine and Jacob and I can't get back to sleep. I'll milk the cows, then I'll take Connor out, and I'll sleep again later. I creep downstairs so I don't disturb Jacob before he needs to be awake.

Before I go out, I open the stove door and throw in a couple of logs. They catch immediately on the embers of the fire that Jacob would have banked up last night before bed. Outside the sun is about to rise above the horizon and the sky in the east is a luminous blue like a magpie's egg. The birds have started tweeting but otherwise there's not a sound. I cross the yard. The slide of the bolt and the clink of the latch on the barn travel cleanly through the cool, slightly damp air. Inside, the cows are stirring, rustling the thick bed of straw beneath them. Their big chocolate eyes reflect the light coming in through the door behind me.

'Morning, Anna, morning, Agnetha,' I say in a low voice so as not to startle them.

Milking is easy once you know how but it did take a bit of practice. You squeeze the top of the teat by the udder, then sort of roll down the teat with your other fingers to squeeze the milk out. It comes out in fast jets that tinkle as they hit the steel of the pail. When I've finished, I take a pint or so off for me and Jacob and pour the rest into the churn. Mrs Beaton's son comes from the village shop for it.

Back in the kitchen I take down the heavy skillet from the hook above the stove and lay it on the hotplate, the fire below it crackling away nicely, then I fetch the bacon. We keep bacon, milk, butter and things like that on the marble slab in the scullery off the kitchen, which is against the north wall of the farmhouse so it's nice and cool.

I lay six rashers across the bottom of the hot pan, and they sizzle but they don't recoil and curl in on themselves like the bacon you get from the supermarket. I cut four hunks of bread and then flip the bacon, gently pushing the fat down on to the surface of the pan to crisp it up. When it's done there's enough fat from the bacon left in the pan to fry a couple of eggs each. I make coffee in the stove-top pot and toast the bread on the hot plate. And just as it's ready, Jacob comes down the stairs.

'I made breakfast.'

'I see that,' he says. 'Thank you very much.'

He thinks I'm not looking, but I see him glance over to the stove to check I've taken the frying pan off the heat. It's not unusual for me to forget, or to leave a tea towel on the hot plate. More than once I could have set the place on fire.

'You'll be wanting a quiet day after yesterday. And you're up early.'

'I'm OK. I'm going to take Connor out, then I'll have a rest later.'

'Right you are.'

I've decided to go up to Granny Carne's. I want to tell her

about the mine. If anyone would know about it, she would. I know there's also a part of me that wants her to say it was all right for me not to tell Jacob. Or maybe she'll say I should have told him, and then I'll have to, I think.

'You could pick up a cake from Mrs Beaton on the way back. We finished that lemon drizzle. No bother if you don't remember. And get the *Echo*, will you?' That's the local paper, the *Times & Echo*.

'Definitely,' I say. That's both of our favourite, lemon drizzle, although more often than not we get fruit cake because it lasts longer. I take a scrap of paper from the sideboard behind me, write 'lemon drizzle' on it and crumple it up loosely, pushing it into my jeans pocket. It scratches my leg slightly. Hopefully it won't get too squashed so I'll still feel it later and it'll remind me. Actually, if I go to the shop on the way I might be more likely to remember and I could get a cake for Granny Carne too. Yes, I'll do that. Granny Carne prefers fruit cake, like most old people, I think.

I have to do little reminder notes for everything now and put them where I'll see them or, in this case, feel them. It doesn't always work but it helps. Memory is a strange thing. I can be thinking about something I want to remember, repeating it to myself over and over, then something distracts me and it vanishes like a candle being blown out. They said my memory was in the bottom 2 per cent of people when I was in the rehab centre. It has improved since, but I often wonder how many things have happened or been said that I just don't recall.

I get my backpack, put a bottle of water and my notebook

into it and head out to get Connor. I take my binoculars too. Mum gave them to me to look at the boats and the birds years ago, and Jacob brought them here from my flat.

'Bye then,' I say to Jacob.

'Sun cream,' he says back.

'Oh yeah, thanks.' I don't bother with sun cream usually as I'm already quite brown but I put a bit on my face if I'm going to be out for a while. The sun here is so much stronger than it is in Bristol. That doesn't sound likely, with Bristol not being that far away really, but it's true. It's because of the sea and how the light reflects off it. I noticed the difference as soon as I moved up there.

'Now I'm off,' I say after rubbing some of the cream on to my face and neck. 'See you later.'

'See you.'

Connor knows straight away that we're going out. He does a sort of impatient jig on the spot with his hooves. This is how he is whenever we set out somewhere, like a pan about to boil over. Then he settles down again once he's burnt off some of his energy.

I put on his saddle and bridle. Niamh looks at me in a way that I understand to mean *And what about me?* If Niamh could speak I imagine she would have a gravelly voice, and grand like a countess. She's very handsome.

'Jacob will be round for you in a bit,' I say, and she looks away. I stroke the side of her nose and lead Connor out, mount him and we set off. It's not far to Granny Carne's, so once we've picked up the cakes and the newspaper from Mrs Beaton, we head up the hill away from the sea to let Connor open up a bit. There's a bridleway that goes all the way to the top of the hill and you never meet anyone else on it as it's so overgrown and not much good for walkers, so we canter up without worrying about someone coming the other way. The dry undergrowth rustles as Connor's legs swish through it.

At the top there's a granite boulder the size of a small car that people say was put there by Neolithic people. How they know that, I don't know. It makes me think about what the land would have looked like back then. Mostly the same, I imagine, but not so many hedgerows and fields perhaps. I like the fields here, how they're laid out. There's no big square shapes like you see in those aerial photos of farmland. They're higgledy-piggledy. You can't flatten a granite landscape or carve it up into neat plots. You have to work with how the land is.

Although it's hardly any distance up the coast, I haven't been back to St Ives since I've been here. I should really, there's people I'd like to see, but somehow I just don't want to. Maybe because it's so busy nowadays and I don't like crowds or noise. I get disorientated and my head starts hurting. Or maybe it would be too much of a reminder of how life was before my cardiac arrest.

From here I can't see a single person for miles around. A buzzard hovers low in the sky almost on a level with my eyeline. It's close enough for me to see its brown and white dimpled belly with my binoculars. It begins to fly in sweeping circles, slicing the air like a sharp oar cutting though water, rising up on the warm thermals. He's searching for prey, a field mouse or shrew perhaps.

Connor shifts impatiently on the spot.

'All right,' I say as I press my heel into his flank. We walk back down the hill as it's not safe to go any faster on the way down. This also lets me look at the detail in the hedgerows as we pass. They are densely packed with gorse and blackberry brambles scattered with all sorts of wildflowers. My mum loved wildflowers, so I know them all, their names carved too deep in my memory to have been dislodged by the brain injury.

I have the idea of picking a bunch for Granny Carne, and I hop off Connor. There are small yellow trefoils, known as 'butter and eggs' because of their buttery yellow petals and orange stamens; papery hot-pink-red campions and hairy willowherb; Yorkshire fog, wheat shaped heads that are soft as fleece; orange and red crocosmia like jets of fire amongst the green; delicate violet herb robert that could be from a fairy garden; purple clusters of lesser knapweed; pale purple sorrel; blooms of water parsnip shaped like those fireworks that explode into huge mushrooms of colour; fronds of prehistoric ferns; and many more. I would have put some gorse flowers in too but their spikes are so sharp and hard that it's impossible to take them without secateurs. Still, I think she'll like these. I tear off part of the brown paper bag that Mrs Beaton put the cake in, wrap it around the flower stems and hold them in my left hand as I mount Connor again.

When we get to Granny Carne's, I tether Connor to the post by her gate. There's a water trough there made from a single piece of granite with the date 1827 hewn into it. It's lined with soft green moss and it's fed by the brook that trickles through Granny Carne's garden, running into the trough on one side, out the other and down the hill. It's also Granny Carne's water supply. Jacob tried to get her to have a water pump installed once. If an animal died in the water upstream she could get ill, he told her. 'I've been all right thus far,' she said, and that was the end of the water-pump idea.

The front garden is on a steep slope up to the cottage, and the path runs from one side to the other and back again like the sort of roads you see in photos of mountain passes, zigzagging their way up. The ground in the garden is completely covered in plants and flowers of all colours in a tight weave that hides every inch of the earth beneath. I look up the garden to the cottage. There's a thin stream of smoke rising straight up from the stout chimney. It's white like a jet stream against the blue sky.

'I'll be back in a bit,' I say to Connor.

The gravel on the path crunches under my feet and before I get to the top Granny Carne has come through the open doorway.

'Hello, Jago,' she says, taking my hands, which are holding the bunch of flowers. I feel the strength of her whole body coming into my hands.

'Hello, Granny Carne. I brought you these.'

'What? No cake?' she asks, her bright blue eyes shining.

'Oh yeah, I forgot. I have got a cake,' I say as I follow her into the cottage.

It takes a moment for my eyes to adjust from the sunlight outside. It's not exactly gloomy inside Granny Carne's cottage but it's not full of light like Jacob's kitchen either. There are red velvet curtains over the two very small square windows, which Granny Carne has drawn to keep the sunlight out. It is lovely and cool inside, like sinking into a tepid bath. The walls are very thick bare granite, which makes it feel almost like a cave. Directly opposite the door is the range, which is similar to Jacob's, with a stack of logs and kindling piled beside it. Hanging over it Granny Carne has her shotgun for rabbits and the like. There's one room here and a wooden staircase on the side wall to the left which goes upstairs. I've never been up there but I suppose it's Granny Carne's bedroom, and perhaps another room as well. No bathroom, though. She has a copper bath down here like back at Jacob's and her toilet is outside, in a little lean-to round the back of the cottage, hewn into the rock face where the ground rises up the hill.

Aside from the stove there's a sink – one of those big square porcelain ones. Belfast, I think they're called. There are cupboards above and to either side of it, made of wood, which is varnished or waxed, smooth to the touch and rounded at the edges from years of use.

Under the cupboards above the sink hangs a heavy skillet and a normal pan as well as four teacups which are white with a fine ivy pattern. I'm always really careful in case I break one, but Granny Carne says they are as old as she is and they're unbreakable. There is one hook with nothing on it and that's where Granny Carne keeps her garden mug for having tea outside. It's deep blue like the sea with a big chip on the handle, and she's always putting it down and then can't find it again, like me.

There's small wooden shelves by the window, over the sink, looking out to the garden at the back of the cottage, which slopes steeply away. On the shelves is a very old and battered tea caddy made of tin, black with a swirly oriental design of an elegant Chinese woman with a painted face and red robes, surrounded by gold foliage. There's also a glass pot containing ground coffee, a little dish with sugar cubes, a small jar of Marmite and a large jar of jam with a handwritten label saying 'Bramble', a little yellow tin of Colman's Mustard powder, a tin of Oxo cubes, a bottle of oil, and a salt cellar.

The rest of the room is given over to a small sofa and an armchair, a round oak table and chairs, smooth from age like the cupboards, a little side table by the armchair and a foot-rest as well as bookshelves. Bookshelves everywhere, jam-packed.

Sometimes I pull out a book and read a couple of pages. I can't read much because it gives me a headache and makes me tired, but I like to open a book in the middle to see what's there. A lot of the books are about plants and nature – birds, mainly. But there's a number of novels too, old ones by people like Virginia Woolf. I opened one of hers the other day: *To the Lighthouse*, it was called. Granny Carne saw me looking at it, and said, 'That's our lighthouse, you know, the one in the book.'

I used to watch Godrevy Lighthouse at night from my bedroom window when me and Mum lived in St Ives. When the light would disappear I'd count the seconds until it came back, imagining that I was far out to sea. Sometimes I would bob my head up and down below the window frame to give the effect of the lighthouse coming in and out of sight through a huge swell, and me in a little boat being tossed around in the storm. The idea didn't frighten me, it lulled me to sleep. As I said before, I feel safe in boats.

'There we are,' Granny Carne says, putting the steaming teapot down on to the side table and covering it with a knitted yellow and green tea cosy that has a little hole for the spout and a bigger hole for the handle. The blankets on the sofa are knitted too, or crocheted I think it's called. She has a basket by her chair with wool, needles, and other things I'm not very familiar with. Sometimes I just sit there while she knits, listening to the soft clicking of her wooden needles. That's another thing that happened with this brain injury. I can just sit and not think about anything at all. As I said, before all this I was restless, but now it's like being a child again, just content in the moment.

Granny Carne pours the tea. It's a deep amber colour. She uses proper tea leaves but no strainer so you end up with a mouthful at the end of the cup if you're not careful. Sometimes she swirls hers around and I think she's reading them, although she never says so.

'You mended that fence.' It's a statement more than a question and I wonder when between yesterday afternoon and this morning she would have seen it. 'Funny business, that.' She pours milk into our cups.

'What do you mean?'

'Haven't you asked yourself who done it?' she asks, sitting back in the armchair and stirring her tea.

'Well, the fence was rotten,' I say, wondering what she's talking about.

'Rotten fences fall apart bit by bit; they don't smash themselves apart.'

I think about this. How had it been when we got down there? I can't picture it but I do remember picking bits of it off the ground to put on to the cart and it's true that the posts and slats were strewn around a bit.

'Oh,' I say.

'Someone causing trouble for Jacob, I shouldn't wonder,' Granny Carne continues, eyes on the knitting she's just started up.

I don't like this. My stomach contracts.

'Why?' I ask.

'Hmm.' Her lips are pursed and her face is sort of tight. We sit there, the knitting needles clicking, neither of us saying anything more.

'What brings you up 'ere anyhow?' she says after a while, her face relaxed again. 'You weren't just passin'.'

I think for a moment. Why did I come up here today?

'I was just bringing the cake,' I say although I feel sure there was something else.

'No,' she says, 'you was going to tell me something, something what's bin botherin' you.'

Then it comes back to me.

'Oh yes,' I say, 'can I tell you something that I don't want Jacob to know?'

'You mean can I keep a secret?'

'Sort of,' I say, hesitating. 'It's just I've done something, nothing bad, but Jacob asked me not to do it, so . . .'

I trail off, not sure what to say next.

'I see,' she says. She knows I'm going to tell her. Her needles click away as I take a breath.

'Well, you know the old mineshaft on our bottom field?

Jacob's bottom field,' I quickly correct myself, feeling my face redden a bit. Granny Carne nods slightly, but doesn't look up.

'Jacob told me not to go near it, said it's dangerous, only I was down in the bottom field yesterday and I was curious. So, well, I had a look. Just at the top of it, I mean, I didn't go down or anything.' I stop and have a sip of my tea. Granny Carne keeps her eyes on her knitting.

'Thing is,' I continue, 'Jacob told me no one's been down it since his great-grandpa covered it up. I mean, no one's done anything to it at all. Not since it was closed up.'

'Hmm.' Click, click.

'Well, the cover on it is new, and the wood's obviously fresh. It definitely hasn't been there for years and years, like not one year even. And there's a new latch and padlock. Shiny, no rust at all. Same with the hinges.'

'Is that right?' she asks, still not looking up.

'So, don't you think that's weird?'

'Well, it is odd, I'll grant you that.'

She pauses her knitting, and looks up at me. I can't read her face at all.

'Praps the council done it, for safety, like.'

'No,' I say, and I know she doesn't think so either. 'The council's got no money for repairing a mine on private land. It's not like it's actually on the public footpath.'

'Most likely Jacob done it and didn't mention it.' She doesn't believe that either, I can see it. There's no way he wouldn't have said anything when we were talking about it.

'He wouldn't be making me promise not to go near it if he had put up a new cover and locked it up, would he?' I don't say this in a challenging way, more like I'm setting it all out for my own thoughts.

'Hmm.' She's looking down at her knitting again.

'So should I mention it, do you think?'

'Who else you seen down there? Anyone?'

I can't think of anyone straight away, but then I remember the other day and the other thing I was going to ask her about.

'No, not down there,' I say slowly, 'but I have seen Bill Sligo a couple of times, walking through the bottom field. I mean, he's allowed, it's a public right of way, just hardly anyone knows about it, so we don't normally see anyone on it.'

'I know that,' she says, not in a patronising way, just factual. I feel my face reddening again. Of course she knows that, she knows everything about this area, like it's all part of her.

'Listen to me,' Granny Carne says, and her voice has changed. There's an edge in it. Not hardness, but something that makes me feel uneasy. She's put her knitting down. 'You stay well clear of Bill Sligo. I mean it, Jago. He's dangerous.'

'Dangerous how?'

My stomach clenches as her face darkens. Her jaw is set now and her eyes have narrowed, but most of all she looks sad.

'OK, I will,' I say quickly, sensing that this isn't a subject to pursue, but I carry on before I can stop myself. 'So do you think he's the one who put the new cover over the mine?'

Granny Carne takes a deep breath, sighs it out, and says, 'Whether he did or not is neither here nor there, Jago. If it was him and you go poking around, he'll not thank you for it. And he's not the sort just to have a quiet word. Do you understand what I'm saying to you, Jago?'

'Yes, I do.'

'All right then. So long as you do.' She looks at me long and steady, and then her face lightens again and the look of sadness vanishes like a morning mist burnt away by the sun. 'Now, what about that cake you was sayin' about?'

'Oh yeah,' I say, standing up and going over to the kitchen sideboard by the sink, glad not to be looking at Granny Carne any more. I've never seen her like that, and I didn't like it, in the same way that I got upset when my mum was sad when I was little. It didn't happen often, but when it did it would feel like a knife through my heart and I would have to do something straight away to make it better, like make her a cup of tea or run out into our little courtyard garden to pick a bunch of oddly matched flowers, thrusting them into a vase and presenting them to her. I'd watch her eyes to see whether it was working, and now I find myself doing the same thing with Granny Carne.

'I'll put these into some water,' I say, picking up the wildflowers that are lying on the side by the cake. I get a small blue vase from the shelf above the sink, fill it up with water and put the flowers in.

Granny Carne comes up alongside me and takes the flowers.

'Look,' she says, 'put the ferns on the outside like this, then they're like a frame for the others, see. Then these, they've got lots of nice leaves to build it out, like, and then these tall ones.' Her hands move quickly as she talks, getting the flowers just as she wants them. She smiles at me and my stomach relaxes. We sit back down and eat the cake, which is packed with fruit and moist with brandy. I want so much to ask more about Bill Sligo, but I know not to.

I suddenly feel very tired. It comes on like this, especially when I've been talking. Tired isn't the word really, and it doesn't describe it properly. It starts with me feeling sick or my head and eyes beginning to ache, and soon I have an overwhelming need to fall asleep. Those are symptoms, though, not the cause. Pathological or neurological fatigue is what the doctors call it. It reminds me of being in the sea when I was little. I'd stay in for hours, swearing I wasn't cold, then suddenly it would hit me and I'd sit between my mother's legs, wrapped in a towel, shivering, teeth chattering, cold to the bone. I need to get back home and rest, but I don't want to go without seeing if Granny Carne needs helping with anything.

'Need anything doing while I'm here, Granny Carne?'

'Not this time, my dear, and anyway, you'll need to go and have a rest now. There's bags under your eyes, dark as thunder.'

'All right then.'

I take the plates and cups over to the sink and rinse them off.

'I'll be off then.'

Granny Carne stands up and takes my hands, gripping them tight.

'You mind what I've said to you,' she says and for an instant that look flickers across her eyes again.

'I will,' I say, squeezing her hands.

'Good boy,' she says, letting my hands go and patting me on the arms, her eyes shining again.

I ride back slowly, my eyes drooping with sleep. When I get back to the farm, Jacob is out. I leave Connor tethered loosely in the shade in the yard, and head upstairs and into bed. The sheets are cool and crisp, and in a moment I'm asleep.

5

It's been five months since Jacob picked me up from the BRI after the surgery and brought me back down here. That's the Bristol Royal Infirmary, the big hospital in the centre of Bristol. I'd had open heart surgery to fix the problem that had caused the cardiac arrest. I don't remember a great deal about it, apart from the pain. So much of what they do in that surgery is so clever and scientific that you can't even think how they came up with the ideas for it, but the start of the surgery is medieval. They saw through your sternum and wrench apart your ribs, holding your chest open with clamps. I knew about that when I woke up. My whole body hurt with a pain that took me over completely. Morphine didn't touch it. Then they gave me something stronger and the pain backed away from me like a wolf into its lair.

The first night I woke and there was a nurse doing something with the special cushion things they put on your legs to stop blood clots. She was trying to kill me, I was sure of it. She laughed and I shouted for help and another nurse came, a kind woman who had rubbed my back earlier in the evening when I was in pain again. I told her that a nurse had come in and was tampering with the equipment; an American nurse, I told her. I was looking out at the ward, but everything was different; I was in a different place altogether. I observed it rather than taking it in. The nice nurse said they didn't have any American nurses on the staff. It wasn't until recently that I realised it had been a hallucination.

The next day was better and I slipped back into the hospital rhythm of meals, blood-pressure checks, heart checks, wound inspections, injections, visits from consultants as well as lots of TV. Repeats of a programme about repairing decrepit old antiques. People brought in stuff like their granny's old teddy bear, and it would be restored and presented to them, and I would well up with happy emotion from all the drugs that were in my system.

After a while they made me get out of bed. I passed out for a moment the first time, but they held me up and got me to take a couple of steps, then the next time it was out to the corridor, then a lap of the ward, then two laps and it went on like that. Sometimes I would pass another person doing their laps in the other direction; we'd nod at each other or say a few words, being careful not to look at the bags of urine we had to carry with us for the catheters to empty into.

I was ten days in that hospital, four and a bit weeks in the neuro-rehabilitation centre before that, and three weeks in the normal hospital before that, one of those weeks in intensive care. It didn't bother me too much for most of the time, until I reached my limit, and I couldn't stay any longer and asked to be discharged.

None of it bothered me, really. It was all just happening. That's one thing with brain injury, or at least it was for me. My brain sort of protected me from the shock of it all by making me unaware of what had happened to me. I knew what had happened in the sense that I was told over and over again until it stuck and I was able to say that I had had a cardiac arrest and had a brain injury. But they were just words with no feeling or understanding attached to them. I was floating along in another world, in another place altogether. My hands moved slowly, I walked like Neil Armstrong on the moon, and I swayed from side to side catching myself on the hospital walls.

I asked whether I could go out for a run when I was at the rehab centre, and the physiotherapist looked at me as if not quite sure what to say. 'Perhaps in a while,' she said eventually. I asked her why not. 'It wouldn't be safe,' she said. After a while she did let me try the treadmill, and I wonder now whether this was her way of explaining it to me. She pressed the start button and within seconds I asked her to turn it off as I was about to fall off it. She didn't seem pleased to be right; she just suggested I stick to the exercise bike.

When I came to the neurological rehab centre it had been snowing, and the air, the first fresh air I had felt for weeks, was cold and crisp on my cheeks. Breathing it in was like having an iced drink on a hot summer's day.

The first couple of weeks in the centre it stayed cold and I kept orange juice on my windowsill so it would be chilled for the morning. Then all of a sudden, in the middle of my stay, spring arrived and I lay on the wall in the garden staring up at starlings swirling and the cornflower-blue sky above. They made me dizzy and I held on to the wall below me. It was in that moment, watching the birds, thinking how they had no idea what had happened to me, that I thought to myself: *Everything is going to be all right. Different, but all right.*

They gave me all sorts of tests and puzzles in the neuro-rehab centre. One day the neuropsychologist came in and told me she had the results. It felt like she was telling me that someone had died when she listed and explained the impairments they had found, not in the sense that I felt sad or shocked or frightened even, but just in her manner. She seemed a lot more bothered than I was. I asked myself whether it upset me, but I couldn't feel anything at all. I still don't feel anything about it, or about anything really. I also never feel excited, or sad, or even bored. Emotional blunting they call it. I do think I understand more than I did though, about what's happened, I mean.

The thing with brain injury for me is that the lists of problems don't mean much to me. I've had to build a relationship with it, to understand what it means, bit by bit. I understand it a lot better than I did, but not completely.

'It's very early days,' they always remind me at appointments, and that feels so odd, so contrary to everything I've known so far in my life about illness. You get ill and, if you don't die, you get better. Normally, you get better pretty quickly, unless it's something bad like cancer, like with Mum. It's different with this brain injury. Things improve, but most of all they change. How I do things now is different.

I can still read and write, for example, but I used to do that without thinking, whereas now I have to focus entirely and still I get things wrong. Now I read and I write slowly, taking my time, so I don't miss words or read or write the wrong word, and no matter how hard I try I still do. I write lists of what I need to do, when I need to do it. I can't cook and do the laundry and listen to the radio like I used to. I can do one thing at a time, and nothing too complicated.

I've gone from someone who needed to slow down, to be present, to having no choice about it. I am slow now; I have to do things separately, giving each my full attention. But I wouldn't change it back even if I could. Not that bit anyway. I was a runaway train before, emotionally anyway, and then there was a monumental and completely silent crash, and everything stopped. My heart stopped and for forty minutes it didn't beat and I didn't breathe. I was suspended between life and death by my friend who gave me CPR by the Bristol docks and the paramedics who, after a final throw of the dice with an injection of adrenaline and three more electric shocks, got my heart to beat again.

But that was only the beginning. I had to pick through the wreckage, blind at first. I had to find all the pieces of me, scattered all around, and put them back together one by one. That's what I'm doing now with Jacob, and the truth is that it's all right. All right, but different.

6

My dream shifts from being in the mountains, to suddenly being in the kitchen of a pizza restaurant on the harbour in St Ives where I worked on Saturdays when I was at school. I wake and hear Jacob in the kitchen downstairs, getting dinner ready. There's still sunlight coming in through the window. It's getting softer as summer winds down, and it's making long oblong shapes across the floorboards.

I watch dust dancing in the shafts of light and I don't think of anything other than the pleasant sleepy feeling in my body. I do a full fingers-to-toe stretch and lie listening to Jacob shifting around downstairs. What was that dream? Yes, the mountains. I try to slip back into it. I've had this dream before, the first time when I was in the coma or shortly after I came out of it, I'm not sure. In the dream I'm in a kind of mountain retreat in Switzerland. I don't know how I know it's Switzerland, I just do. I'm in a big pine-panelled room with huge windows looking out over snowy mountains from high, high up. It's a place for recuperation. I don't know how I know this. There are no nurses or doctors, but I know that they'd come if I needed them. It feels completely pure: not just the mountains, but the feel of the place altogether, like there's no emotion there apart from kindness and calm. I feel safe, like there's nothing in the world to think about apart from that single moment. I sometimes have another dream like this, only I'm in an Irish hospital. I think about it, and I wonder if this is what it feels like to be a baby with a belly full of milk.

The feeling slowly ebbs away as I lie here, but I'm left with an imprint of the dream. I'm full of contentment and I don't want to get out of bed and lose this feeling, but I can hear Jacob starting dinner and I want to help him.

'Hello,' he says as I come down the stairs, yawning. 'You were tired. We overdid it on the fence yesterday.'

I think about this.

'No,' I say, 'it was talking to Granny Carne.'

This is true. Talking or reading is much more tiring for me than physical things. I start to lay the table for dinner.

'How was she? All right?'

'Yeah.'

'Did you get the *Echo*? Don't matter if you didn't.'

'Oh yeah, I did.' I finish putting out the plates and cutlery and the two glasses of water and a couple of pieces of kitchen towel each, and I fetch my bag from by the door.

'There's cake too,' I say.

I lay the newspaper out on the table, and look over the front page. There's something about one of the car parks in St Ives and a planning application to turn it into flats. There are always long articles like this about planning, how every postage stamp of land in St Ives is bought up for development. 'Bad business', Jacob calls it, because it pushes all the locals out. There's another piece about the lifeboat day in St Ives with a photograph of the Coastguard helicopter hovering over the harbour, and crowds pushed up against the railings to get a good look. I loved lifeboat day when I was little. They have it in all the coastal towns with a lifeboat station. You get to go on the boat and meet the lifeboatmen. Everything on the boat would be spotlessly clean and shining, brass knobs glinting in the sunlight, against the blue and orange of the lifeboat, bright and fresh. The other big article on the front page says *Penzance drug gang smashed in dawn raid*. It says the police and the Coastguard have closed down a drug-smuggling route from Spain, and that they are on high alert for the smugglers setting up a new landing point on the peninsula. The policeman they interviewed says they believe there is already a backup landing point so that the supply is not disrupted.

'Anything interesting?' Jacob asks as I'm reading this.

'Not really,' I say. 'Drug smugglers in Penzance got caught.'

Jacob makes an *Aaargh* sound like the sort of pirate who has a wooden leg and a parrot on his shoulder. 'I got cake too,' I say. 'Lemon drizzle again.'

'Lovely. We'll have some of that after dinner. It's sausage and oven chips. No peas.'

He grins at me. He knows sausage and chips is my favourite and how I'm not keen on greens. He doesn't bother trying to make me have them. I used to like greens, a lot. And salads. But the brain injury's changed that.

I get the ketchup, HP sauce, salt and vinegar from

the cupboard and pass Jacob the plates. He puts three fat sausages on to each from the frying pan, and shakes out the chips. Jacob always pours a little pyramid of salt on to the side of his plate and dips his chips into it one by one rather than sprinkling salt over them. I like watching him do this.

'What have you been doing?' I ask him.

'Fixin' that fence.'

I wonder for a moment whether I have misremembered fixing the fence yesterday, and we'd actually only talked about it, but no, I'm sure we did it.

'What do you mean?'

'Someone or somethin' broke it again.'

'They never did. Why would they do that?'

'No idea. Kids, I suppose.'

'Really?' I ask, but it isn't really a question. What kids would come this far along the coast path to break a fence? And why? What would be the point? It wouldn't be quite the same thrill of smashing up a phone box, for instance, would it?

'Is it finished or will we do more tomorrow?'

'We'd better finish it tomorrow,' Jacob says. 'The field's out of use until we do. You needn't help, though. It's no bother, really.'

'No, I will,' I say. 'I liked doing it yesterday. It was satisfying, seeing it done.'

'Maybe that's what you should be thinkin' of for your future, like. Somethin' with your hands. You're strong, even after that surgery, and you'll only get stronger now.'

'Maybe,' I say, 'or maybe working with boats.'

This is something I've already been thinking about. I worked on the boats in Bristol, on the ferries that go between Temple Quay near the train station and the Cottage pub at the other end of the docks. I liked being on the water. It was always so light, even in the middle of winter, and it reminded me of being by the sea. I also liked seeing all the boats every day. The big ships like the SS *Great Britain* and the *Balmoral*, and all sorts of houseboats from great lumbering Dutch barges to narrowboats with beautiful paintwork and covered in pot plants.

The place I liked most on the docks was the Albion Dockyard. It's a proper dry dock where they repair all sorts of boats. They had a beautiful timber pleasure cruiser in there for a long time when I was there. When she was finished she was a golden amber colour with polished brass portholes that gleamed in the sunshine, making her look like she was studded with diamonds. I'd like to work somewhere like that, become a proper craftsman, but I'm not sure that's realistic really.

'Anyhow, all in good time,' Jacob says as if reading my mind, as he lifts a sausage to his mouth and takes a big bite. I don't think we're the best influence on each other, manners-wise.

We don't talk much over dinner. It's often like this. We're both happy with the quiet. When we've finished I take Jacob's plate and stand up to do the washing up, and as I turn to the sink, I see an envelope on the mat by the door.

'There's a letter,' I say, putting the plates back down and going over to pick it up. It's a fancy envelope, thick creamy paper. It says *Jacob Trevarno Esq.* above the address.

'A posh one, too,' I say, handing it to him and going over to the sink to start the dishes.

Jacob goes to the little table by the front door and I hear a neat rip as he opens the letter with his letter knife. He sits back down at the table and I hear him unfold the letter. For some reason I feel nervous, like there's bad news coming. I focus my attention on the cutlery and the plates, washing every piece very carefully. Then he laughs and says, 'The fool.' I wasn't going to ask him what it says, but this seems like an invitation to ask.

'Who is it from?'

'Bill Sligo. His solicitor anyway.'

My stomach twists.

'What does he want?' I ask, trying to keep my voice light.

'Bottom field.'

'He wants to buy it from you?'

'It would seem so.'

'What for? It's not even connected to his land.'

'Not directly, no. But it's connected by the lane, which as you know is public. He's had this idea previous about setting up a stall selling coffees and cakes and whatever else to the walkers on the coast path. Reckons he could make a fortune in the season. Probably could.'

'Probably couldn't,' I say. 'He'd never get planning for that. It's National Trust, the coast path.'

'Well, I don't think he's the sort to make planning applications.'

'That's just stupid,' I say. 'He'd never get away with it. The council would find out in no time and close it down. When did he tell you about this anyway?'

'Oh, quite recently. And that's exactly what I told him.'

'Then he'd be left with a field he couldn't do anything with.'

'None the less, he's willing to pay a pretty penny for it. Look.' He hands me the letter. The paper is thick and cream coloured. The letterhead says *Chapman, Crawley & Wrath Solicitors*. I start reading.

'You can skip the first part. It's all guff. Bottom of the page.'

Mr Sligo is willing to pay the sum of twenty-five thousand pounds (£25,000) in addition to reimbursing your reasonable legal costs, on condition of completion taking place within a month of the date of this letter.

'Twenty-five thousand sounds a lot for a field that you couldn't get planning for, isn't it?'

'Yes, it is.' Jacob is looking at the letter again. His expression is sort of distant.

'He'd have to sell a lot of cakes and coffees in the few days before the council shut him down to make that worth it,' I say.

'He would. But he won't be sellin' anything from that field, not while I'm around.' Jacob says this almost to himself, still with that distant look on his face.

'You're not selling, then?'

'No, I'm not selling.' His voice is slightly raised, firm not angry.

'How can he afford it anyway? His farm isn't very big, is it?'

'He's got money. Don't ask me how, but he has. Have you seen his car?'

'I don't think so,' I say, trying to think.

'Great big bloody Range Rover with cream leather seats. That ain't the sort of vehicle you need for farming. Ridiculous.'

'I wonder where the money comes from?'

'Wheelin' and dealin'. He's a shady one, is Bill Sligo.'

'Like a criminal?' I ask.

'He's had enough brushes with the law, but nothing that ever stuck. He's a nasty piece of work. Violent. So you stay clear of him, you hear me?'

'That's what Granny Carne said too,' I say.

'Yes, well, I shouldn't wonder.'

'What do you mean?'

'There's bad blood between them.'

'Why?'

'Well, that's for her to tell you if she wants to.'

'All right,' I say, seeing there's no point in asking more. 'I'll get the cake.'

There are two things that make Mrs Beaton's lemon drizzle so good. One is how moist it is, almost dripping with sugary lemon syrup, like a rain cloud about to burst. And the other is the sugar crust on top, which cracks like the surface of fresh snow that's frozen overnight. I cut two slabs, and put the kettle on to the hot plate.

'Do you want to play some chess?' Jacob asks. He's been

teaching me to play. I'm not good, and it's tricky because of these visual things I have. I can only see part of the board at once, for instance, so often I get surprised by a piece coming out of nowhere, and I often forget what I was thinking, or what the last move was. Sometimes I even forget whether I'm playing white or black. I still like it, though, mainly because it's nice playing with Jacob. He could have been a teacher in another life. In a school, I mean. He's patient and encouraging, and just nice.

I pull over the red armchair so I can sit opposite Jacob, and he takes the chess set from the sideboard. It's a very old wooden set with carved pieces that are tall, slender and noble-looking. The wood is soft and worn and each piece has a little emerald-green disc of felt stuck on the bottom so they slide smoothly over the board. They look very small in Jacob's hands. His hands are big and strong, but he lifts the pieces delicately, placing each one precisely on to the centre of its square.

'Here, try this,' he says, 'it's two-move checkmate. White to move.'

We often do puzzles like this. Jacob sets out a problem and I try to find the solution. He says a lot of chess is about patterns, which worried me a bit because I can't really see patterns, or imagine what the board would look like two moves ahead or whatever. One of the things I have is called aphantasia. It means I can't visualise things in my head.

'The more we look at these things, the more they'll sink in,' Jacob says. This is another thing about him. He knows what my problems are, but doesn't see any reason why we shouldn't play, even though one of the neurologists thought it was too much. They don't want you to set yourself up for failure, that's the thing, but I just like playing with Jacob and I don't care whether I'm good or not.

I shift my gaze around the board, trying to work out what the move might be, but I can't.

'I can't see it,' I say after looking for a while longer.

'OK. Well, look, here it is. It's not obvious at all, so I'm not surprised you didn't see it. It takes a long time to see these things.' He shows me the move and then looks up at me. 'Anyway, actually I think we're both really tired. Let's stop for today.'

The water left in the kettle is still hot enough to wash up our plates and the sausage pan. Jacob dries and puts the things away, and we both go up to bed, Jacob putting out the oil lamps behind us.

It's almost dark in my room, the window a square of dusky purple. I light the candle and long shadows stretch out from it. I take my bible from my bedside table and open it at the bookmark.

Jesus looked up and saw the rich putting their gifts into the offering box, and he saw a poor widow put in two small copper coins. And he said, 'Truly, I tell you, this poor widow has put in more than all of them. For they all contributed out of their abundance, but she out of her poverty put in all she had to live on.'

I start to read but my eyes are too tired. I close it and watch the candlelight making the ceiling sway. I think about what happened today. I can't think what I did this morning, but then I remember Granny Carne and her warning about Bill Sligo, and the letter and the fence being broken again.

All of these things are connected, I think, but I'm not sure how. I need to think about it again tomorrow, so I'll write it down. I take my notebook from the drawer and write *Granny Carne, Bill Sligo, Letter* in a list. I put the notebook open on my bedside table where I will see it in the morning, and blow out the candle.

7

It's late when I wake up. Half past ten. I'm still tired from visiting Granny Carne and talking yesterday. Fatigue is like a bruise. Once I've got it, it doesn't just go away after I've rested. It fades slowly and only if I'm careful. That's why I have to try not to get too fatigued in the first place. I must have slept for eleven hours or more last night, but I'm tired, my head hurts and I feel sick. Days like this drag on. I should feel better than this tomorrow if I'm careful today; it's something I'm still getting used to. It takes time to get used to not being able to do whatever you want whenever you want. I stayed too long at Granny Carne's. I knew it at the time, but it's hard to stop before it's too late, when before all this I could be talking all day, no problem.

There's no sound at all in the farmhouse. Jacob will have started his day hours ago. I look again at the travel clock on my table and I see my notebook next to it.

> *Granny Carne*
> *Bill Sligo*
> *Letter*

I remember writing them down. But what do they mean? Another thing that I thought about just as I was falling asleep was the fence. Obviously it's Sligo trying to make

Jacob think the bottom field is more hassle than it's worth so he'll sell it.

He won't sell it, though, I'm sure of it. This land has been in our family for more than a hundred years. If Jacob won't sell it, and Sligo wants it so much, then what does that mean? What's going to happen? He can't make Jacob sell it, can he? I need to find out why he wants it so much. If it's some of his shady business, as Jacob called it, maybe he can be stopped. I don't know how I'll find out what he's up to, but I know what I'm going to do first. I'm going to go up to Blackheath Farm – Sligo's farm – and have a look around. I'll go today. I can just make out I'm going out for a ride on Connor.

I pull on my clothes, splash my face with water from the jug by the corner sink and go downstairs. Jacob's breakfast things are already dry on the draining board. I can't be bothered to cook anything so I'll just have toast; there's lots of bread still from yesterday. I cut three thick slices and lay them on the hot plate. We don't have a toaster so this is how we do the toast. When it's done I spread butter thick, and then spoon on bramble jam. Jacob made this and it's more liquid than shop jam. It's sweet and an oily purple colour. Jacob says we will make some jam together when the blackberries are ready. It won't be long now; the tight clusters of green berries are already turning deep rosy pink all along the hedgerows.

I finish my toast, rinse the plate and knife, drink a glass of water and go back upstairs to brush my teeth and get my bag. I put in my notebook and binoculars, head back downstairs and wrap up a slice of cake in waxed paper.

Connor is impatient to get going when I open the stable door. Niamh isn't there. Jacob will have her with him and he would have expected that I'd be taking Connor out.

Bill Sligo's farm is long and thin, stretching back inland like a finger. The track from Jacob's to the sea also runs inland, past Blackheath and all the way up the hill and over to the other side of the peninsula.

I pull on my wool jumper before hoisting myself up on to Connor. It's overcast and the air is cool and damp like there's a fog rolling in.

'Come on,' I say to Connor and he sets off. It's a gradual climb all the way up towards Blackheath, getting steeper the closer we get. Although it's not far from Jacob's, the land is wilder up here, most of it heath rather than farmland, with heather covering the ground instead of grass, and granite boulders rising out of it in places as if scattered by giants. The wind sweeps off the sea and up these hills, bending the gorse and heather so that it hugs the ground like someone's run a comb through it.

Sligo's farmhouse is at the end of a long private lane and hidden behind a ridge so I don't see it until I'm almost on top of it.

'Whoa,' I say softly to Connor. The clouds above are now thick with heavy purple bellies. Light glows in the windows of the bottom floor of Sligo's farmhouse, even though it must be almost noon. From up here, on this ridge, I have a view of the house and the land around it. The grass surrounding the house grows in wild clumps, patches of dried mud in between and all sorts of junk lying around. There are dozens of tyres of all sizes, piled up to one side of the house; a rusting old gold Ford Cortina raised up on bricks with no wheels; a quad bike that looks newer; petrol cans; messy nests of rusting barbed wire; a tractor that looks like it's from the 1950s or before; piles of scrap metal, ochre with rust; and three other cars: Sligo's Range Rover, a black Mercedes and a red BMW. I look over the house, checking to see if there's anyone outside but there's no one there.

I pull my backpack around and take out my binoculars.

'Steady,' I whisper to Connor as I lift the binoculars to my eyes. It takes a moment to find the windows amongst the granite blocks of the house, but then my line of sight lands on one and I can see inside. The only thing visible from this angle are the flagstones of the floor inside. It's hopeless; I'll have to wait until they come out.

I jump off Connor and lead him back a few paces to where he's out of sight. Then I crawl back to the ridge so that only my head pokes out over the parapet. I can quickly duck down if anyone looks up this way. I take the cake from my bag and start eating it, while I look around Sligo's yard to see what else is there. Really there's just a load of old junk. The farmhouse doesn't look much better. The roof is thick with mustard-coloured lichen and the paint on the window frames is blistering and peeling away. It's a solid house, though, the granite-block walls much like Jacob's and Granny Carne's.

I watch the birds through the binoculars. There aren't many. Some larks, with squat bodies like fighters, and thrushes with their well-to-do upright postures. No birds of prey, though, which is a shame, as they are my absolute favourites.

I'm losing focus and my mind is drifting when the door opens and three men file out, the bulk of Bill Sligo at the back. The first man has a shaved head and is younger than Sligo, maybe thirty. The other man is older with a long greasy grey-brown ponytail. This one lights a cigarette. They are talking loudly and some of their words drift up to me. I can just hear the bald one say, 'I'm telling you, they'll go with someone else if we're not ready soon.'

'We'll be ready.' This is Sligo.

'Enough of this,' says the one with the ponytail as he starts to walk back towards the Mercedes. I stuff the binoculars into my bag and crawl back to Connor, stand up, jump on to him from one of the boulders and squeeze his flank. We need to go, otherwise they'll catch us up in the lane in no time, and what excuse could I give for being here? The last thing I want is for Sligo to know I've been watching him.

'Quickly,' I say to Connor, giving him a gentle kick with my heel. It's not safe to go too fast on these lanes, though, in case a car comes around a corner ahead, but we go as quickly as I dare. I can hear my own breath, short and ragged. Then I hear the engine of a car behind me. It's getting closer. We should have waited, we should have hidden, I think, and let them leave first. Why did I not?

'Easy,' I say to Connor, 'it's OK.'

The car is behind us now, too close. I glance back. It's the BMW. The driver is revving his engine, but there's nowhere for me to let him pass, and he knows it.

There's no need to panic. He's not going to drive into us, but still my heart is pounding and I can hear my breath.

'It's all right,' I say, as much to myself as to Connor. I

smooth his neck, still holding the reins in both hands. He'll be OK so long as I stay calm. The car's horn blasts behind us and the engine revs again. He's far too close to us. I mustn't let Connor speed up, though, as if I do, I know this man will chase us and then Connor will scare and bolt. I glance back again and see the man's face sneering. He's enjoying this. I feel sick. The horn goes again. There's still no sight of anywhere to let him pass. The lane is only just the width of a car. He wouldn't drive into us, surely? There's another blast of the horn. I hold the reins tight and glance at the white of my knuckles. The car revs again, and again.

And then I hear it, the chug of a tractor, as it appears around the corner in front of me. Thank God.

I lean forward and shout to the farmer in his cab, 'Please help me.'

I see the farmer look beyond me and clock how close the car is to us and I know he understands. He starts to reverse and as I follow him around the corner I see a passing point by the side of the lane. The farmer beckons me on and I pull up beside him.

'This man's driving right behind me, blowing his horn, I don't know what he's doing. I've got a brain injury. I don't know what to do.' I'm overwhelmed and I've got tears in my eyes.

'You're all right,' the farmer says. 'Where are you going?'

'Jacob Trevarno's farm. Near Towednack. He's my uncle.'

'I know Jacob,' the farmer says. His face is worn, and folded like all his skin has been scrunched up. It's a kind face and he has clear blue eyes that tell me he's going to sort this out.

'You carry on home,' he says, 'and I'll keep that bastard at bay.'

'Thank you,' I say, 'thank you very much.'

As soon as he's gone, I know I should have asked his name, but I'm not thinking straight.

We pass the tractor quickly, and I hear him drive towards the car, blocking the passing place. That BMW will have to reverse a long way now and it will take a while.

'Walk on,' I say to Connor, 'walk on.'

I push him into a gentle trot, thinking even if the farmer delays him, that man in the BMW will still catch up with us. Instead of coming up with ideas, as I would have done in the past, my mind is blank, and the harder I try to think, the less I'm able to. It's like being in a dense fog where whichever way you look you can't see anything. I feel tears gathering in my eyes again. I hate this: my mind is paralysed and I don't know how to get out of it.

And then the answer comes without me doing anything – a gap in the hedge on the left, leading into a field. I guide Connor into it and immediately we're hidden from the lane, the dense bush of brambles, ferns and the rest too tall for anyone in the car to see over, and far too thick to see through. *What if he finds us in here, though?* I think. Well, he couldn't drive over this field, could he? No. Is there a way out? I look around. Yes, there is. In the top corner of the field is another opening. Maybe I could go by the fields back to Jacob's farm instead of the lanes. I expect I could, the only thing being whoever's farm this is might not take kindly to it. I think of the man prowling around the lanes in his car. I'd rather face an angry farmer than see him ever again.

'Come on,' I say to Connor and we start to make our way up the field. All the way I have a feeling of being chased. I used to have nightmares about it as a child — being followed by a stranger and no sound coming out of my mouth when I tried to shout for help. I'm not going to look back, though. When we get to the top I will. I haven't heard any cars passing. We carry on.

At the top I glance back and there's nothing there. In the next field another track goes round the perimeter of the field and we follow it, and then the next, and then the next. Since the brain injury, my sense of direction is really bad, but so long as we are heading downhill I know we will be going towards the coast and Jacob's farm will be there somewhere.

I feel tired now and suddenly I'm very hungry and thirsty. We stop by the next gate and I jump off Connor and sling my backpack around. I sit on the grass and pull out what's left of the cake, eating it quickly, then lying back. The grass is so long and dense it's like a mattress. I stare up at the sky. The thick clouds have passed off now and a scattering of giant cumulus clouds like skyscrapers drift slowly across the sky, expanding and shrinking as if breathing, their wispy edges dissolving into the blue sky beyond. A couple of gulls soar in sweeping arcs high above me.

I am calmer now, but still my mind goes back to that car and that man. Why was he doing it? Was he just one of those nasty people? One of those idiots who likes to goad a horse, or did he know that I had been up at Blackheath? At this thought my stomach knots. If he did know, and that's how he reacts to it, there's definitely something going on. Those men are doing something they don't want anyone else knowing about.

I get up from where I'm lying, restless with worry, and needing to get going. At the top of the next field there's a farmhouse, some outbuildings and a barn. There's no way around it; we're going to have to go straight through the farm. I hope they don't mind. It looks very much like Jacob's farm, low-lying buildings hunched down to stay out of the wind. Granite walls with thickets of fern sprouting out here and there. It's not as up together as Jacob's, but it's not neglected either. There are bucket-sized terracotta pots either side of the door overflowing with pansies and snapdragons. Hanging beside the door is a brass bell, tarnished by the weather. Just as I'm coming to the house, the door opens, and a small, slightly plump woman steps out, wiping her hands on her apron. I swing my leg over Connor and jump down on to the heavily worn cobbled courtyard.

'Hi,' I say.

'Hello,' she says, a slight smile lifting the corners of her mouth.

'I'm sorry to bother you,' I say, and before I can continue I feel my throat tighten and tears filling my eyes. I pinch my nose at the top by my eyes to stop myself crying, but I can't.

'I'm sorry to bother you,' I say again, 'I'm not normally like this. I've got a brain injury.'

I feel ridiculous.

'Oh dear,' the woman says. 'You'd better come in.' Her voice is warm and friendly. 'You can tie him over here,' she says, pointing at Connor and walking towards a trough by the far wall of the courtyard. I do as she says and follow her inside.

'Here, sit down.' She pulls out a heavy wooden chair from around the table. The arms and back are smooth and shiny with wear. She puts her hands on my shoulders. 'A cup of tea, I think,' she says, 'and a couple of these. I've just pulled them out of the oven. I'm Betty by the way, and this is Hawthorn Farm you've stumbled across.'

She turns to the range and picks up two scones from the baking tray and brings them over on a plate, which has a fine rose pattern painted around the edge. My crying has stopped as quickly as it started, and I already feel better. This woman reminds me of my grandma, sort of cuddly, although I wouldn't say that, obviously.

'Thank you very much,' I say. 'I'm Jago Trevarno. I'm sorry, I don't usually cry, it's just something that happens with this brain injury I've got – I just get emotional sometimes, and it sort of washes over me.' It's called emotional lability, but I'm not getting into that.

'Better out than in,' she says, 'but something set you off, surely. What's happened?'

And the whole story spills out of me, even the spying on Bill Sligo and the men I saw with him. I don't know why I tell her all this. I wonder for a moment whether she might laugh at the whole thing, at me, as it's already sounding stupid as

I'm saying it. She doesn't, though. She looks at me with a steady gaze throughout as if she's really listening to me.

'That does sound the sort of person Bill Sligo might be havin' dealin's with. He's a rough sort, that one.'

'You know him then, Bill Sligo?'

'Oh yes, he's our neighbour unfortunately. There's not many round here don't know Bill Sligo, or know of him, I should say, as I'm not sure anyone actually knows him. He's a loner and a rough sort, as I say, and not someone a nice young man like you should be getting mixed up with.'

'I have to know what he's doing,' I say, looking straight into her eyes. They're milky grey, almost silver.

She takes a deep breath before saying, 'And what do you imagine he's doing?'

'I don't know,' I say. 'That's what I want to find out.'

'Well, the truth is, that man is a drug dealer. Everyone knows it, even the police, but nothin's ever stuck. He's clever. Cunning, if you will. And dangerous. Oh yes, mark my words, that man is a menace. He wouldn't think twice about doing someone in who gets in his way, as would the men he hangs about with. Nasty lot.'

She stands and goes over to the stove, picking up the large metal kettle and topping up the teapot.

'Have another scone,' she says. 'You look half starved.' She looks at me, sort of appraising me, like a mother would. 'I've just put it together. You're Jacob Trevarno's nephew and you've been ill, haven't you? Your heart, wasn't it?'

I don't bother to ask how she knows. I've thought before about how news passes through this area and I've drawn imaginary red lines in my head connecting Mrs Beaton's shop to every farm and cottage around like the strings on a map in one of those police drama programmes on the TV.

'Yeah,' I say.

'And that's what caused the brain injury, is it?'

'Yeah,' I say again. Sometimes I'm wary of people who ask. But her face is soft and she doesn't have that greedy look people get when I know that they're listening but at the same time thinking about who they'll tell this to later on.

'My heart stopped and I wasn't breathing for a long time, so my brain didn't get the oxygen it needed.'

'Oh dear.' She almost whispers it, her eyes glistening. She reaches over and takes my hands in hers. 'You're here now,' she says, rubbing my hands. 'And thank God for that.'

It's almost dusk when I eventually leave, stuffed full of scones with another half a dozen in a brown paper bag in my backpack.

We talk about what happened to me and about her life. Her brother had a heart attack not much older than me. We talk about farming life, how losing some farming subsidy almost forced her and her husband to sell up, how they carry on by letting out wooden cabins that her husband built to holidaymakers, how she sells her scones and jam and her huge range of pickles. 'If it can be pickled, I'll pickle it,' she said, laughing, and she showed me her store cupboard with shelves all up each wall completely full of jars of all shapes and colours: blackberry jam as dark as ink; terracotta-coloured chutneys speckled with mustard seeds; and piccalilli almost as bright as my best T-shirt when I was ten which turned fluorescent yellow when I was hot. She tells me how the roof needs to be retiled, but no quantity of scones or pickles is going to pay for that; how they had always thought their son, James, would take over the farm, but he'd injured his leg in a motorcycle accident so now he has an office job as an insurer which he doesn't really like, and a girlfriend from Exeter who she, Betty, doesn't really like.

She draws me a map to get home without having to go back the way I came, a simple one that she says I can't go wrong with.

'Or you could wait for Joe,' she says, 'and he'll show the way, but he'll be a while yet.'

I say I'd better get going as Jacob will be worrying if I'm away any longer.

'You're a good boy,' she says, and she rubs my arm before I jump up on to Connor. Her hands are strong, full of work. 'Come again,' she calls after me as we walk out of her yard.

Once we are round the corner, I give Connor a nudge in the side to get him going a bit. I don't mind riding in the dusk or even at night; I like it, the feeling of the dark pushing in around me, the sounds and smells of night which are so much more vivid than by day. I don't want to ride on these lanes in the dark, though, but we'll get back before then if we get a move on. It's not good for Connor to go too fast on tarmac, but a steady trot is OK.

I turn my mind back to this afternoon and to Bill Sligo being a drug dealer. It makes sense. You don't buy cars like his with the income from a small farm that's almost entirely idle. And the police couldn't pin anything on him, Betty said. I wonder why not, especially if everyone knows about the drugs, which she said they do. And how much of what happened today should I tell Jacob? How much does he know already? I'll tell him about being at Hawthorn Farm — I'll just say I got lost — but I'm not telling him about going up to Sligo's farm or the man in the car.

He'd worry about that a lot.

8

'Time to get up.'

Jacob is jiggling my ankle from side to side.

'What time is it?'

'Seven, I'm afraid. We leave at eight, so you've plenty of time.'

'Leave where?' My eyes are still closed. I haven't been sleeping well since that horrible trip up to Bill Sligo's farm a week or so ago.

'Truro. It's your appointment, remember? Nine o'clock.'

I remember now. It's in my diary and on the calendar in the kitchen, but if Jacob wasn't on top of things, I'd have carried on and not thought about it until the next time I had seen it written down. And I mustn't miss this as the consultant is coming all the way from Exeter for it. Brain injury from cardiac arrest is her specialism.

'You're very interesting to us,' she had said on the phone, and she wasn't the first to have said that to me.

'Why do people say interesting?' I had asked, and the line had gone quiet for a moment before she said, 'Partly your age. You're very young for a cardiac arrest, and you articulate your difficulties very well.'

I understood what she meant then. Most people who have a cardiac arrest die. Then there are those who are so badly brain damaged they are in permanent residential care. And then there are those who are resuscitated very quickly, and spend no time or little time in a coma. They might have problems with memory and fatigue, perhaps, but they seem to go back to work quite quickly and go out socialising and that sort of thing. I only know this because there's an online group for 'survivors' that I was told to look at. There wasn't a single person on there with a brain injury like mine: severe, but not so bad that I can't function. That's what she means by interesting. Not so damaged that they can't get any sense out of me – not now at least – but damaged enough.

We don't talk much in the car. I watch the hedgerows turn into verges and then we're on the A30 heading up country. It's odd to see all these cars, and the people in them. All the drivers driving without thinking, just doing it.

I'm tense with anxiety. I try to read the signs as we go but I can never get to the end of them as they pass by in a blur. A car overtakes and pulls in so close to us that I grip my knees and breathe in sharply, but Jacob doesn't flinch. Tears well up behind my eyes. I'm not sad. I'm overwhelmed, and my head hurts. Luckily, Jacob has his eyes on the road so he doesn't see this. I close my eyes and take deep breaths. Six seconds in, six seconds out, one, two, three, four, five, six. Six, five, four, three, two, one.

I wake up with the motion of the car going round a roundabout.

'We're a bit early,' Jacob says, glancing over at me. 'Want to get a tea or something?'

'I don't think so.' I like to be early, to sit for a bit in the waiting room, check if I've got everything I need, that sort of thing. Really I just need my notes – medical notes, I mean. I'm on the second ring binder now. Hospital discharges, neurological reports, cardiac reports, surgical reports, blood tests, letters from specialists. They don't write to me directly, they write to each other about me and send me copies. They refer to me as things like *this pleasant right-handed gentleman*, or sometimes they say *polite* instead of *pleasant*. I think it's a sort of code they use, letting each other know whether they've got a difficult patient on their hands. I requested all of the records from when I was in hospital. They sent hundreds of pages of them. I haven't been through them all yet, but I had a quick look at some of the nurse's notes from after I came out of the coma.

Moody and sarcastic this morning, one of them wrote one day. It made me smile because although I can't remember it, I can imagine that being true. Not that I am rude to people. The opposite, I think, but I can imagine lying there, confused and fed up. Another thing with brain injury is that it affects your filter. Sometimes you say things that normally you would stop yourself from saying, but they just spill out. I don't think the nurses minded. They've seen it all.

We're pulling into the car park now. Jacob goes to pay and I check my bag is done up. Neurology departments are quiet, I've found. They have an old-fashioned feel. There's also something academic-feeling about them. Neurology feels like a higher art, not like cardiology which is quite macho in comparison. And when I think about it that makes sense. The heart is mechanical and electrical. It holds no mystery. But the brain is so unlikely. Flesh like the rest of the body, but able to create hopes and dreams, love and desire, ideas and actions. It's also the great unknown, that much has become very clear to me. So much of how the brain works is not understood. 'The mechanism of fatigue is not well understood,' I was told once. I wanted answers in the beginning, concrete answers. My main question was: *When will I get better?*

'There's no end point to neurological recovery,' the consultant had said. Another said two years is the 'sweet spot', the point when the long-term picture becomes clearer. Everyone seems to say the same thing, more or less. The fastest recovery is in the first six months, then the first year, and after that recovery can continue but it's slower and it slows down even more as time goes on. But what does that mean for me? I always want to ask. 'Every brain injury is unique,' they say. 'No two brain injuries are the same.'

But what does that mean for me? I wonder again.

The waiting room is busier than I expected, but then this isn't a neurology department. There are people here with broken legs and wheelchairs; someone sitting with a drip.

My head already hurts from the strip lighting overhead. It would be good if they could make waiting rooms like living rooms at home with armchairs and soft lighting. I feel nervous too; I always do before these appointments. It's something to do with authority figures, I think, like being called in to see the headteacher and watching the expression on her secretary's face to see whether she'll give anything away about how bad it's going to be. It's stupid, I know, particularly because the other thing about neurologists is that they're nice and kind – all those I've met have been anyway – and they just want to help.

'Jago Trevarno?' I look up as the consultant calls again but I can't see who is speaking. Then they wave and the motion of their arm catches my eye, because if I'm not looking straight at someone I can't see them.

'I'll be here, shall I?' Jacob asks.

'No,' I say quickly. 'Can you come in with me?'

'All right.'

We go into her room, and she smiles a kind smile at me, the consultant, and gestures for us to sit down.

'You've been through it, haven't you?' she says, looking down at the folder on her desk. 'You're lucky to be alive.'

'Yes,' I say.

'Yes,' she says again and it sounds almost apologetic. Then: 'What date is it today?' she asks.

'Thursday,' I say after a pause.

'Yes, Thursday. And the date?' she asks.

'I'm not sure,' I say. 'Beginning of October.'

'It's the nineteenth of October today,' she says. 'What's the name of this hospital?'

'Um, Truro?' I say, not sure again.

'Does it have another name?'

'Not sure.'

'What floor are we on?'

I can't remember.

She asks me to repeat an address after her, and says she'll ask me about it again later. Then she asks me to count backwards from one hundred in sevens, which I can never do. She holds up her hand and asks me to copy her as she opens and closes it, and twists it around. She asks me to draw a clock pointing at ten to ten. She asks me which is supposed to be the long hand, and which the short.

'Can you tell me what these are?' she asks, holding up images of things like brooms and rolling pins.

'What was the address I asked you to remember?' she asks a bit later on.

'Orchard Street, Devon,' I say, my eyes hot with tears again.

'Any other parts of the address?'

I know there was a whole lot more but I can't remember any of it.

We carry on like this, with lots of little tests, until I push my hands against my eyes and she puts down her pen.

'That's enough; you're tired. And how are you feeling, generally?'

'Very tired all of the time. Right now my head hurts and I feel sick.' Tears roll out of my eyes and I cover my face with my hands.

She comes closer to me on her chair. It's one of those spinning ones with lots of wheels. She puts her hand on my knee.

'None of this is your fault,' she says.

We talk for a while longer. I keep forgetting what I'm saying as I'm talking to her, but she doesn't mind. She talks about strategies for coping, and she says she'll see me again in six months.

I don't know why I got emotional. I wasn't sad. I just sometimes get these waves of emotion when I talk about how things are and how everything has changed. And this is odd because most of the time I don't feel emotions at all. They call it apathy, pathological apathy. It's like my mind is the surface of a lake on a windless day. No waves or even ripples, just a steely unchanging surface. I'm not happy, and I'm not sad, not excited or bored: just the occasional rushes of tears, and then back to nothing. It sounds bad, but it's not really. Actually, I think it's helped me. People say to me how awful it must be what's happened, but I don't care about it. I'm fine floating along in the middle.

I feel content as we leave. The consultant has made me feel valid. The thing with brain injury is that if you look at yourself in the mirror, you would never know anything was wrong. Even to talk to I seem fine, at least to people who don't know me.

'You have to be careful,' they said to me in neuro rehab. 'You present well. You have a strong veneer. Your injury won't be obvious to people.'

I think that's why I feel content as we leave the hospital. I felt understood, whereas most of the time I feel alone because as nice as people are, they don't understand. Even Jacob doesn't understand, not really, but he doesn't pretend to either, and I especially like him for that.

People often say things like 'Oh, I know that feeling, my memory is awful too', or 'Everyone forgets things', or 'Oh, I know, I'm always exhausted'. I just smile. It's like telling someone you have a tumour and they tell you about a bump on their head from knocking it the other day. No, it's not as bad as that, but it does grate. And I know people are just trying to be nice but I think I'd rather they just didn't say anything at all.

The doctor today has calmed me and, as we sit in the car, I feel lighter than I have for some time. I start to think of Bill Sligo again and a plan comes into view in my mind in the way that things do when you stop thinking about something for a bit. I need to know more about him and I realise, as if I've known for a while, that my plan is to go into St Ives to the library to look through the local newspaper archives. If he has had these close scrapes that the farmer's wife was talking about, surely there will have been something about it in the local news. I have it in my mind that the way to get Sligo to stop hassling Jacob is to get something on him. And with this decision I fall asleep for the rest of the drive back.

I sleep again when we get home and I wake slowly to the sound of Jacob in the kitchen. I hear something else too, a folk song, something very old as if I've slipped through a hole in time. My mind is back in the coma. It's dark but I hear something far away as if I'm at the bottom of a well. Deep male voices chanting a language I don't know. The words carry me like waves coming in and out over the shore. There are other sounds too: a metallic banging, over and over again, beeps and a chain rattling, all of them muffled. I have a sense of being underground. I can see the walls in the little light there is, and they're black brick, wet with dripping water. Somewhere further off, the sound of an underground train clattering through a tunnel.

And then I'm back in my room, the light outside fading to dusk. I don't move at all. My body and mind feel cocooned in warmth and comfort. I don't have a care in the world. There's just this moment, this feeling of complete safety.

As the noises downstairs become clearer and my surroundings come more into view I think about the feeling and where it comes from. I've had it before when my mind has slipped back to a time in the coma or perhaps when I woke from it. I don't know how I know that that's what it is, but I'm sure of it. I've had a sort of dream – only it's so real – of being in a hospital in Dublin, cared for by young nurses who I liked so much even though I didn't speak to them. I don't know why it would have been in Dublin, I just know somehow that it was. I think again about where the feeling comes from, what it means. I think it's from those days after the cardiac arrest when my body had nothing to do but live. My mind had retreated deep below the surface of consciousness and was drifting slowly through a kaleidoscope of senses, like a leaf spinning on the surface of water.

After a while I put on my dressing gown. It's getting cooler now and the boards under my feet are no longer softly radiating warmth at the end of the day. I splash some water on to my face and go downstairs. I see Jacob's broad back at the sink. He's solid, like an ox as they say. And calm like the oxen in the stable in Bethlehem, I think as I come in and I half laugh at the thought of it which makes Jacob turn his head to look at me.

'All right, sleepy head,' he says. 'Sausages again, that OK?'

'Perfect,' I say. I keep meaning to cook something. The idea floats in my head, wavering between thought and action, unable to make it over the line. I go to the sideboard and take a couple of plates and put them in the warming oven in the range, then get place-mats and cutlery and two glasses of water. The water comes straight from the pump outside the kitchen and it's as sweet as any other drink.

'How you feelin'? That was quite full on at the hospital, wasn't it?'

'I'm OK. Bit tired, but fine.'

'You'll want a quiet day tomorrow.'

'Yeah,' I say, and then I remember my plan. 'Although I was thinking I might go into St Ives tomorrow?'

'No,' Jacob says in a drawn-out sort of way, 'but I tell you what. You help me harvest the patches out the back tomorrow and you can come with me to the farmers' market the day after and have a mosey around then. How does that sound?'

'Good,' I say.

'Right, well, that's settled. Should be rain tonight,' he says, looking up at the sky through the window. 'It'll soften the earth a bit. Less resistance from the carrots, you see,' he says, giving me a wink.

This is another thing I like about Jacob. The smallest things make him happy.

'Go on then, sit down,' he says, piling mountains of steaming buttery mash on to the warm plates and ladling over his onion gravy. It's thick and sweet with juniper, his secret ingredient.

'That'll put hairs on your chest,' he says, putting three sausages on to my mash and one more sticking out of the top. The gravy simmers with tiny spheres of juicy fat from the sausages, and in the middle of the table is a bowl of cabbage cut into ribbons, deep earthy green. I'm stuffed at the end of it but I eat every bit, even the cabbage.

'I think I'll have a bath, if that's all right,' I say after washing up and seeing that the boiler is still more than half full. I'd meant to have one yesterday before seeing the doctor but I forgot.

'Go ahead.'

I take the copper bath from the scullery and put it by the range. Then I pull out the screen we use as a sort of privacy wall and put it alongside the bath. It's a wooden frame around a faded Japanese pattern printed on to cotton. I fill the copper bath with jugs of water from the boiler as well as topping up with cold and I lower myself into it. It feels good to be sitting in the warm soapy water.

'I'll put on a tape,' Jacob says from over in his armchair and I hear him flicking through his shoebox of cassettes, and putting one into the machine. It's an old battery-powered one shaped like a thin brick with an opening that pops up so you can slide the tape in and push the lid back down. We mostly listen to Rowan Atkinson comedy sketches from the 1980s and '90s. Jacob laughs out loud, full-throttled belly laughs. The sketches are funny, but it's Jacob's laughing that mostly gets me going too. I sit until the water is just tepid; then I empty it out and go up to bed, very tired. I look at my little travel clock by the bed. It's half eight and it's dark. I blow out the candle and wait for the stars to prick through the night sky outside the window as my eyes adjust.

I wake in the night, rain hammering on the slate roof above me. I like the sound of it. I feel safe and cocooned in my iron-framed bed. I think of the shipping forecast on the radio and how my grandpa used to have it on late at night in his bedroom, his mind far out to sea with the sailors.

Irish Sea – variable 2 to 4, becoming north-east 3 to 5 for a time. Smooth or slight. Fair. Good. Shannon – east or north-east 3 to 5, becoming variable 2 to 4. Slight or moderate. Fair. Good.

9

When I wake properly, a shaft of sunlight cuts across my room, speckled with billowing dust that shimmers like flecks of gold leaf suspended in water. I get out of bed and look through the window. Everything is soaked and new, the bushes heavy with beads of water glistening like Christmas tree baubles.

'Good bit of rain, that,' Jacob says when I come into the kitchen. 'Reckon those carrots and potatoes will be jumpin' out the ground.'

We eat our breakfast and go out into the veg patches behind the farmhouse. The earth is a deep brown like dark chocolate and it sinks like a sponge as I put my boot on to the first furrow.

There's the late potatoes that Jacob left in the ground, but also carrots, autumn cabbages, huge and sprawling like triffids, and early Brussels sprouts on tall stalks like medieval studded clubs.

I push my fork into the earth and it sinks softly into the ground. Jacob has shown me not to dig too close to the plants or you hit the potatoes and they split. I heave at the fork gently, lifting the plant like it's on a hinge, and below, connected by the finest tendrils, the potatoes are revealed with their bright purple-pink skin like precious pebbles, all different sizes. Occasionally I do split one, and its white flesh dazzles in the autumn sunshine. I like it when I find huge potatoes and I lift them up shouting for Jacob to look. I'd have thought the novelty would have worn off for him a long time ago but he shouts back things like 'Cracker' or 'That's a big bugger'. It's easy work when the ground is so soft. The more daring birds swoop in behind us to snatch up the worms that are still writhing in the upturned earth. We fill one wheelbarrow with potatoes, then another. There's probably another couple of barrows' worth in the ground, but Jacob says we'll let them dry in the ground as there's no more rain forecast for now, then we'll lift them and store them for ourselves.

Next is the carrots. They come up easily too. They're good straight carrots because Jacob uses a poker-type thing that he pushes into the ground with the seeds so that they have a sort of sinkhole to grow down into.

He uses a big knife like a machete to cut the cabbages. One swipe at the stalk and they're off. Same with the Brussels, which we leave on the stalk rather than picking off each one. Jacob says people prefer buying them like that. They stay fresher for longer.

By the time we've finished, we have four sacks of potatoes, a sack of carrots and a lot of cabbages and sprouts too. At the farmers' market tomorrow we're also going to take eggs and chutneys and pickles from Granny Carne. Jacob picked them up from her the other day.

'Do you think we'll sell it all?' I ask, thinking that it's a lot of potatoes for a farmers' market.

'Most of it, I shouldn't wonder.'

I try to calculate in my head how much money that might make for Jacob. One sack of potatoes weighs a hundred pounds. If we sell them in three-pound bags at £2.50 each, what would that be? I try to work it out, but as soon as I move from one number to another my mind freezes and it's like I'm staring at a concrete wall and can't get around it. Hopefully it will make what he needs anyway – he doesn't seem concerned about it. If Jacob had his way, there wouldn't be money at all. People would trade what they had and help those who didn't have anything.

Once we've finished, we wipe down the forks, oil them, and put them away in the barn; then we stop for a cup of tea, sitting out the back looking at the freshly dug patches, the sun already low and casting long shadows in the furrows. My boots are caked in mud and heavy like a diver's lead boot. My back, legs and arms ache pleasantly and the air tastes sweet as I take in deep belly breaths and sigh them out again.

I feel good and I realise that most of the time I don't. Most of the time I'm tired, but not in the fulfilled way I feel now: tired like I'm dragging a sack of sand behind me. Like everything is an effort and I have to force myself to do even things that I know I like doing. But in this moment I feel the fatigue of the day, not of months, and I savour it. Maybe this is what I should be doing with my life when I'm better. *Better.* I catch myself on the word. It's not one I like. In the beginning, I thought of being ill and getting better and that's how things normally work, isn't it? You get ill and then you get better, or if you don't, you die. You don't just float somewhere in between, at least I didn't know you could. I never thought about it because why would you when you're well and healthy and running from one thing to the next, never thinking about your heart or your brain.

My heart is better, though. The surgeon heaved open my chest and fixed the valve like a plumber replacing a washer on a leaky tap. But what about my brain? I am impaired. My vision is impaired, my memory is impaired, how fast I think is impaired, I struggle to multitask, I can't read and write as I did, I can't do maths as I did, my mind freezes when it gets overloaded, which doesn't take much. But I don't mind any of it really. Well, I don't like being tired and sick all the time, or the constant struggle to motivate myself, but I know now that I won't ever go back to how I was, and I don't mind that.

In the same way that I can no longer drive or cycle, and I walk or ride Connor everywhere instead, so it is with my brain. After Mum died I was speeding along on autopilot, never pausing to look around. I was trying to get somewhere, but I didn't know where.

Now I'm on the footpaths and bridleways, walking or riding Connor, my eyes free to roam around. Now I'm sitting with Jacob, watching the steam from my tea rising up and dissolving into the air, looking at the leaves that are a little crisper than they were a few days ago, a little closer to falling, a little closer to winter.

'You look good,' Jacob says. 'You've got a good colour.'

We sit until the sun slides behind the trees leaving a slight chill in the air.

'Right,' Jacob says, 'we'll load up the cart and then we're done.'

It doesn't take long. We wrap the jars of Granny Carne's

pickles and chutneys in hessian sacks and wedge them between the sacks of vegetables. It's a decent load overall.

After that's done, we go back inside and have beans on toast, thick with butter and Marmite, and then I'm ready for bed at eight.

I leave Jacob putting the animals down for the night and head up to bed, too tired even to brush my teeth.

10

I wake from a deep and dreamless sleep to the sound of Jacob down in the yard. It's very light in my room. I've slept too long. Jacob must be going to St Ives without me. I get out of bed, put on my clothes and rush down the stairs and out of the door. Jacob's there, checking the straps on the cart.

'Wait for me.' I hear myself sounding like a little boy.

'I am,' he says. 'Just wanted you to sleep for as long as you could. There's toast and tea on the side – bit cold, like, but it'll be all right.'

Soon, we're on our way, Connor pulling the load easily. Niamh is down in the bottom field for the day. It would normally be Niamh pulling the cart but it wouldn't be safe this far into her pregnancy.

The sky is a soft pale blue without a cloud and the air is cool, sweet and very fresh. A few degrees colder and the glistening beads on the dew on the grass and bushes would be thick with hoar frost. I take a deep breath down into the bottom of my lungs and exhale like a steam train.

It's almost three miles into St Ives and it doesn't take too long to get to the market in the Guildhall. We unload while a couple of impatient drivers honk their horns. This doesn't bother either of us. I think before I would have felt the tension rising, felt harassed and rushed to clear the road. Now I don't care. Once we've finished, I mount the cart and ride out of town to Bramble Farm. Jacob knows the people there, and they let him leave Niamh or Connor and the cart whenever he likes, like a sort of car park for horses.

'It'll be pretty crowded and noisy in here in a bit,' Jacob says when I get back to the Guildhall. 'You go for a potter around. Come back for three and I'll be done.'

Jacob also gives me a list of a few things to pick up from the hardware shop. It's right opposite the library so I'll go to the library first and get the things later. He wants four pounds of three-inch screws amongst other things that I don't want to carry around all day.

I like the smell of libraries. It's not the same as a bookshop with that new-book smell. It's more homely, as if the books have picked up little bits of scent from each home they've been in and it's all mixed together here. The librarian at the desk looks exactly as a librarian should. She's got on a cardigan and she's wearing big bifocal glasses on a gold chain that loops down the side of her face and around her neck.

I tell her that I'm looking for old copies of the *Times & Echo* and ask whether they're in a database so I can search them.

'No, dear, I'm afraid not. They are on microfilm, though, if you want to have a look through?'

I say I would please and she shows me to the machine, which must be at least forty years old. Beside it there are small wooden drawers, labelled alphabetically, and she pulls one out to show me the microfilm.

'Here,' she says, sounding pleased. 'These are the *Times & Echo* arranged by year. Now, be careful not to mix them up; it's best just to take one out at a time and put it back once you finish with it.'

'Thank you very much.'

'I'm over here if you need more help.'

I look in the drawer she has opened. It's about two feet deep and packed with black plastic slivers of microfilm separated with dividers, each marked with a year. Where to start? I have no idea, so I just pull one out and slot it into the machine. With the slightest move of the handle, months of pages fly by as fast as newspaper coming off the printing press. I use much smaller and smoother movements to slow it all down, and individual pages start to come into focus.

I see stories about planning-permission grants; a fire in the baker's; good exam results from the local comp – my old school; a renovation of the artists' studios overlooking Porthmeor Beach; a new family-run Italian restaurant opening on Fore Street. This is hopeless. It's like looking for a needle in a haystack blindfolded. What was I hoping for, a load of articles about Bill Sligo to pop out at me? I sit back in the chair and sigh, staring at the screen, my eyes and head already aching just from this short period of scanning and reading.

'Any joy?' It's the librarian, her glasses chain tinkling as she leans forward and peers at the screen.

'No,' I say and I hear the dejection in my own voice.

'What is it you're looking for, if you don't mind me asking?'

'I'm not sure exactly,' I say, wondering how much I

should tell her. For all I know she could be Bill Sligo's sister, although I doubt it somehow.

'I'm doing some research on drug crime in West Cornwall, especially in these parts,' I say carefully.

'Well, your best bet is Roger Minack, in that case. He's a reporter for the *Echo*. Been at it for decades. He knows everything worth knowing about any goings-on around here.'

'Great, thank you,' I say, feeling more optimistic already. 'Where would I find him?'

'Try at the offices. Of the paper, I mean. It's on the High Street, behind the chemist, you know?'

'I know. Thanks very much. You've been really helpful.'

'You're very welcome,' she says, looking pleased. I replace the microfilm in the long drawer and head back outside. The chemist is only around the corner, so I stop on a bench before going down to the offices to think what I should say to this Roger Minack. I decide to be upfront with him. The worst thing that can happen is Sligo finds out I've been asking about him, and that's not the end of the world. And people normally respond when others are straightforward with them. I think so, anyway.

The newspaper office is nestled away down a shoulder-width alley behind the chemist in a small building that once would have been a fisherman's cottage. I push open the claret-red front door and a bell dings. The inside is panelled with pine slats with the wall to the left covered top to bottom with shelves stacked with stationery: diaries, folders, notebooks, single envelopes, packs of envelopes, stickers, packs of pens, rolls of parcel paper. It reminds me of shopping in Woolworths for back-to-school stationery with my mum. I think we would have come here if we'd known about it.

There's no one here and I'm about to call *hello* when a woman appears from the back room. She looks friendly.

'Hello,' she says, 'can I help you?'

'I hope so,' I say. 'I'm looking for Roger Minack.'

'Aren't we all?' She has the easy laugh of someone who laughs a lot. I must look confused because she straightens her face and says, 'Sorry, love, just jokin'. He's elusive, you see. Could be anywhere, although your best bet is out the front of the Sloop. Great big moustache. If he's there, you'll see 'im.'

'Thank you very much,' I say, surprised at how straightforward that was, and I head back out. The Sloop is the pub on the harbour, opposite the post office. It's ancient. There's supposed to have been a pub on the site since 1300 or thereabouts. I like the old history of St Ives, imagining men fishing back then and drinking in the pub and barrels of salted pilchards being traded on the harbour slipway outside.

It's only a short walk round the harbour to the Sloop. If this was the summer holidays it would be heaving with every seat taken and people spilling out into the harbour. But it's quiet now, and the stout man I see when I get there can only be Roger Minack. He's sitting on one of the benches with a half-drunk pint of ale, a pipe sticking out of the corner of his mouth through a bushy nicotine-yellow moustache.

His face is mahogany brown and deeply furrowed. He's wearing a faded navy-blue fisherman's cap, and the hair beneath it is white and wild as if the hat is only just managing to contain it.

'Excuse me, are you Roger Minack?'

'Might be,' he says, but his tone is playful and the corners of his mouth twitch slightly.

'I'm Jago Trevarno,' I say. 'The lady at the newspaper office said I'd find you here. I'm doing some research and I was hoping you might be able to help me. Can I get you a drink?'

'Go on then. Put a half in there,' he says, holding out his glass. 'Can't promise I can help, mind.'

'That's all right,' I say. 'What are you drinking?'

'She knows,' he says, nodding towards the pub door. I get his pint topped up and myself a ginger beer and head back out of the gloom of the pub into the light outside.

'Cheers then,' I say as I sit down opposite him and lift my glass.

'Good health. What are you, a journalist? Writer?' He examines my face.

'I'm not really anything at the moment,' I say. 'I'm not well, so I'm not working.' He doesn't ask what's wrong and I appreciate that.

'What is it you're trying to find out?'

'Well, I live with my uncle up at the Trevarno farm. My uncle is Jacob Trevarno. Do you know him?'

'I don't, but I know Trevarno farm. I knew Morgan Trevarno – your grandfather, I suppose?'

'Yes, that's right.'

'But I don't know you, do I? You lived there long?'

'No, just since I've been ill. I'm from St Ives but I was living in Bristol for a while before then.'

'I see.'

'So, I've been at my uncle's and he really helped me a lot. He *is* helping me a lot, I mean.'

Mr Minack pulls on his pipe, waiting for me to carry on. The smoke from it smells sweet, nothing like cigarettes.

'Well, there's this person who lives up the hill from the farm and the thing is . . .' I pause, thinking how to carry on. 'The thing is, I think he's trying to cause trouble for my uncle.'

'And you want to help your uncle, because he's helping you.'

'Yes. You see, when I say I've been ill, I mean really ill. I had a cardiac arrest. That's when your heart stops all of a sudden.'

'I know,' he says.

'Oh, right,' I say. 'It's just that most people think it's a heart attack but that's not the same thing at all.'

He nods at this and waves his hand a little to say I should carry on.

'Well, I've got a brain injury from not breathing for a long time when it happened, and I haven't been able to go home to Bristol or back to work. So, my uncle kind of saved me really.'

'Sounds like you're a lucky man.'

'In some ways, yes,' I say. 'In some ways, no.'

'And the person causing trouble?'

'Bill Sligo. He lives up the hill from us. He wants to buy one of our fields, Jacob's fields I mean, and I don't really understand why. He doesn't need it or anything; it's not even connected to his land, not directly. But I've heard things about him and I'm worried he's up to something and he's going to drag my uncle into it somehow. Have you heard of him?'

'Oh yes,' he says, 'but why have you come to ask me about him?'

'I don't know, really,' I admit.

'And what does your uncle have to say about him? He'll know a bit about Bill Sligo, living down the hill from him, I'm sure.'

'I haven't asked,' I say. 'I know my uncle will worry if he thinks I'm trying to get involved, so I haven't told him. I just think it would be a good idea to know more about Bill Sligo's intentions.'

'Your uncle would be right to worry, and if Bill Sligo wants one of your uncle's fields, my advice would be to sell it and be done with it. Your uncle's got plenty of other fields, I'm sure.'

'But what if he doesn't want to sell it – which he doesn't, by the way.'

'That would be a mistake, in my view. Mr Sligo is a nasty piece of work, and I don't mean he's a bit rough around the edges. He's bad through and through, and if he wants something, he won't be fussed about what he has to do to get it.'

'That makes him sound like a murderer,' I say without really thinking.

Mr Minack takes another long draw on his pipe and looks at me as if trying to decide something; then after a moment he says, 'If the cap fits.'

It takes a beat for this to sink in.

'What?' I say and I hear the shock in my voice.

'I'm not telling you secrets here. This is well-known stuff. A few years back – well, quite a few, ten or perhaps twelve – there was a disagreement in the Tinners Arms. You know it?'

'Yes, in Zennor, it's not far from us.'

'That's right. Well, that night, Sligo got into a disagreement with a young man called Cadan Carne over—'

'Hang on,' I interrupt him, 'Carne as in Granny Carne?' I feel stupid as soon as the words come out of my mouth, in calling her Granny Carne to him, even though everyone seems to call her that.

'Morvoren Carne. That's right.'

'The man was her son?'

'No. He was a lot younger than that. Her sister's grandson, so her grand-nephew I suppose. But they're all very close in that family, so he may as well have been her son, especially with her having no children of her own, like.'

'What happened?'

'Well, by all accounts there was a set-to in the pub. Not much to it, they say. There was a bit of chat going on in the bar, a bit of a debate, like. No one's particularly clear on the specifics. Fact is, they'd all had a couple too many. Anyway, this discourse ended up with Sligo and the Carne boy squaring up to one another. They were pulled apart and things settled down. Sligo left shortly after and that seemed to be the end of it.

'Only the Carne boy didn't come home that night. His mother raised the alarm and a search party was got together. But they didn't find him. He'd been drinking, as I say, so it was assumed he'd fallen asleep under a bush or something and he'd be back all sheepish, like, in the morning.' Mr Minack takes a sip of his beer. 'However, he didn't come back, and next morning his body was spotted by a couple of walkers down on the rocks below Zennor Head, skull cracked open. Well, of course the official story was he had walked down there for some reason, to clear his head perhaps, and he slipped. No one believed that for a minute. He wouldn't have gone there in the first place. Why would he? Besides, he was from around here. He wasn't about to slip off a cliff like some clueless emmet.'

'So what happened then?'

'Nothing. Police came, of course, and you had the boy's family and various others fingering Bill Sligo, but what proof was there? Sligo had left the pub a good hour or more before closing; there was nothing unusual on the Carne boy's body, no marks that couldn't have been made by the fall. His body was quite a mess by all accounts. "Accidental Death" was the coroner's verdict. Such a casual term, isn't it, when you think about it. Caused quite a stir at the inquest, I can tell you.'

'You were there?'

'I was: I was covering the story. The mother screamed at the coroner. "Accident?" she shouted. "He was killed by that murdering bastard Bill Sligo." Well, we had to be a bit careful about how we reported that one. Didn't want to get done for libel. Anyway, that was the end of it as far as the law was concerned, but not for the boy's family and a lot of other people. For them, Sligo had got away with murder.'

'And do you think that too?' I ask, a slight chill having taken hold of my body.

Mr Minack doesn't answer straight away, but sips at his beer and then wipes his moustache with the back of his hand.

'Well, it's as likely as not. Fact is there was no reason whatsoever for that young man to have been down on the coast path and Sligo is a nasty bastard, no doubt about it. And if it was Sligo, that's not to say he actually meant to kill the boy, but he might have.'

'Blimey,' I say. I need to think about it all, let it sink in, try to understand what's been said and what it might mean.

We talk a little longer, but not about Bill Sligo, just chitchat. Then I'm about to leave and I remember the other thing I was going to ask.

'Sorry, one more thing.'

'Go on.'

'Is Bill Sligo a drug dealer? Someone told me he is.'

'That's what they say,' he says, 'but he's a slippery one.'

And with that I cut back along Fore Street with Mr Minack's words going round and around my head. *If he wants something, he won't be fussed about what he has to do to get it.*

11

Fore Street in St Ives is the high street, and it's mainly shops for the visitors, not useful things really, but it's nice to look in the windows and I always like to see if any of the shops have changed. Firstly, there's the shell shop which is like an Aladdin's cave for children, packed with baskets of shells – pointy worm snail shells like tiny unicorn horns, scallops, brown spotty tiger cowries and huge conches with their spiky armour. And loads of crab claws that always gave me the creeps, although I always liked the ships in bottles on the shelves. Further on, the camera shop is still there; I can't remember it ever not being there. And now, on my right, my favourite shop.

I'm glad it's still here. I used to come with my friends just to look through the window, which had a sort of grate over it, adding to the feeling that it was forbidden. Then, when we got a bit older and bolder, we would go in and just look at everything until the shopkeeper would ask if we were actually planning to buy anything and we'd leave, but then do the same thing a few days later. I wanted everything in there. BB guns, potato guns, air rifles, catapults. Especially the catapults.

The one catapult I really wanted was the Black Widow and it came with an arm rest – so you got some real power into the elastic when you pulled it back – and a pack of ball bearings. I would lie in bed thinking about it, longing for it really.

There was no way my mum would have let me get one, though, so I saved up my money secretly, then asked my friend Stevie's brother to get it for me as you had to be sixteen to buy one. Me and my friends would take it down to the harbour in the evenings if the tide was out and line up Coke cans for target practice. It was so powerful that the ball bearings would pierce the cans. We would do that day after day until the sun went down and we had to go home to bed.

And when I wasn't actually using it, I was thinking about it. It was around that age that I became aware of how my mum was wary of men after dark. If we were out for whatever reason and there were drunk men around the pubs, I could hear the tension in her voice. She was distracted and not really focusing on whatever it was we were talking about. So, after I got the catapult, and if we ever went out in the evening, I would take it from my hiding place under the loose floorboard in the corner of my bedroom and have it in my jacket pocket just in case. So, although the catapult was mostly for fun, it also made me feel that I could protect my mum if I needed to.

Anyway, here it is: the shop. I can remember now exactly how excited I would feel when I went in there. That's a funny thing with this brain injury. I can remember things from years ago as if I am living them right now, but struggle to remember what I did yesterday.

I wander along Fore Street, looking at the Halloween displays in the shop windows, and I'm almost at the end when I hear someone calling my name. I turn to look where it came from and see an arm waving. And then I see her just as she was the last time I saw her, her dark brown wavy hair bouncing as she comes out of the bookshop towards me.

'Sophie,' I say in a rush and then stop. I'm not sure whether to hug her or what, but she steps forwards and holds me tight.

'It's so good to see you,' she says into my ear.

When we let go of each other, I look at her face and see her emerald-green eyes are full of tears.

'I've wanted to come and see you, but I didn't know if you'd be ready,' she says.

'I've been wanting to see you too,' I say. 'I'm sorry I didn't tell you I was back. I don't really know what I've been waiting for.'

'Come in. I'll put the kettle on,' she says.

'All right,' I say. 'I'm meeting Jacob at the Guildhall, but not for about an hour.' And I follow her into the shop.

I've been coming to this bookshop for all my life, and the smell of it makes me think about coming in here with Mum, but also of all the times I've been in here with Sophie, while she served customers and restocked the shelves or whatever else it was she was doing.

She closes the door behind us and flips the sign to 'Closed'.

'I wrote to Jacob,' she says as we go into the little room at the back piled high with books and boxes of boxes, but also a kitchenette.

'He didn't say.'

'No. I asked him not to. I sort of wanted to see you when

I saw you, if that makes sense,' she says, filling the kettle and taking down two mugs from the shelf above it.

'When did we break up?' I ask, and straight away think what a stupid thing that was to say. It's just that since seeing her in the street I've been trying to think exactly when it was, but I can't.

She looks at me and her face isn't annoyed, it's more sad.

'You can't remember,' she says.

'Not really,' I say. 'I mean, I can remember it, but I can't place it in time. It's the same with loads of things, as if everything's all jumbled up like a jigsaw.'

'That's OK,' she says. 'Hey, remember all the jigsaws we used to do?'

I do remember. We used to sit in the back corner of the pub doing big jigsaws and making our drinks last for ages as we had hardly any money.

'Yeah.'

'Is it scary?' she asks.

'What?'

'Not being able to remember things?'

'Oh, no, not really. It's just weird.'

'Can you still surf?'

'Not at the moment. I tried, but my balance is all off.'

'Oh,' she says and I know without her saying anything that she understands what that means for me. I've always surfed, me and my mates, and with Sophie too, and her friends. It's just what we did. The weather didn't matter; we'd always go out so long as there was surf.

'So when was the last time you remember seeing me?' she says.

'Well, it was just before I left for Bristol, so what's that? A year and a half ago?'

'Yeah. Christmas, year before last.'

'After the storm,' I say as fragments of memory flicker through my mind too quickly to see them properly. But then the detail starts to come back to me.

That year, in the week between Christmas and New Year, we had the most almighty storm. The whole sea was white with foam and looked more like a field of snow than the sea, and it was heaving up and down, left and right, all over the place really. The waves were the size of houses and they slammed into the beach and the cliffs, sending up huge plumes of spray.

It raged from the afternoon and all through the night, finally passing early the next morning, although the wind was still wild. I met up with Sophie that morning on the harbour where the shop- and restaurant-owners were sweeping water out on to the street and stacking the used sandbags. The storm surge had been so big the sea had come right over the harbour wall. We walked away from the harbour down the Digey and when we rounded the corner by Porthmeor Beach, the wind took our breath away as we grabbed on to each other.

We couldn't believe it when we saw the beach. It had changed shape. All the sand had shifted and was banked high up against the flats. The deck where the café put out tables and benches was gone, leaving just the tops of the posts that had been driven deep into the sand, now standing bare like tree stumps after a forest fire.

As we walked along the beach it felt as if we were being

pushed back by an invisible hand, and when we tried to speak our words were swallowed by the wind. It wasn't until we reached the mound of rocks further on that we could take shelter and hear each other. From there we could see up to the beach huts that all been smashed in, windows broken and doors missing or hanging off their hinges.

'I've been thinking,' Sophie said. 'We need to be honest with ourselves. It's not going to work, you being in Bristol and me being here.'

It didn't worry me, her saying this. We'd had this conversation many times over the past few weeks, each time ending with us saying we'd work it out. I would visit on these weekends, and she would visit on those.

We were sitting side by side with our backs to the rock, looking out to the sea, which at low tide was much higher up the beach than it should have been. It wasn't until I turned to look at her that I saw something had changed, and panic start to rise up in me.

'I won't go then,' I said, shifting round to face her.

'Yes, you will,' she said and I could barely hear her through the wind, the crashing waves and the pounding of blood in my ears. 'You need to go or you'll never move past your mum dying.'

'What?' I said, but it was an impulse, a stopgap, as I didn't know what to say.

'Going away is the right thing. I've been thinking about it and I can see it all clearly now. You need a clean break from everything here.'

We carried on talking like this, half shouting to hear each

other, pulling on opposite ends of the rope, until I could see there was no point.

'So that's it then?' I said.

'For now, yes.'

'What does that mean?'

'Well, no one knows what's in the future, do they?'

We didn't talk on the way back along the beach, but we held on to each other tight, partly because of the wind but mainly because we were afraid to let go, I think. The trouble was we loved each other, which made it all so much worse.

The next day I got the train up to Bristol, and I didn't see her again until now.

'In some ways that seems like yesterday,' I say, 'but also like it was years ago. As I say, nothing's in the right place any more.'

Sophie doesn't say anything to this but has a sip of her tea. She's just the same as she was. She won't say something for the sake of filling a silence. She looks just the same too, with all the hair that I'd get lost in when I held her and that always smelled of coconuts. There might be a couple of new rings on her hands, which are always brown, even in winter. She makes her own jewellery, mostly out of silver, and sells it too. One of her rings, my favourite one, is modelled on the mermaid of Zennor from the carving in the church in Zennor.

She gave me a silver bracelet before I went to Bristol, but I caught it on a cleat on the ferry in Bristol and it slipped into the water. I saw it almost suspended in the green water and I plunged my hand in after it, but it had gone.

'I missed you, you know,' she says, looking straight at me.

It's not an accusation, a precursor to asking why I haven't been in touch. She's not like that. She just says what she feels; there's no hidden meaning behind her words. It was one of things that I first liked about her. I was always quite guarded about my feelings, keeping myself to myself, so she seemed bold in comparison.

'Me too,' I say.

'You never called or wrote after you left,' she says.

'I know,' I say.

If this had been before the brain injury I don't think I would have said anything else, but now I don't see the point in not saying it. It doesn't feel dangerous any more.

'The thing is,' I say, 'I knew that if I spoke to you when I was in Bristol, I'd have come straight back. I wanted to come back as soon as I got there, but I just couldn't be in St Ives, not after Mum died. And then I also wanted it to work out.'

'And did it?'

'I don't know. I mean, I had a job on the ferries, and a couple of mates, but a lot of it is just a blur.'

'Do they think your memories will come back?'

'Probably not.'

'But you remember us being together?' Sophie says, and I can see tears in her eyes again.

'Of course. It's most of the year before the cardiac arrest that's gone. The rest is there, I think, on the whole. But it's mixed up, like I said. But of course I remember us being together.'

Sophie makes more tea and we sit in silence for a while with the faint chatter of people wandering past outside. I think we always liked this about each other, that we could just be together like this. We used to lie in bed for whole afternoons, watching the shaft of sun from the window creep over the floor.

'You know I didn't want to break up; that wasn't why I left,' I say.

'But you did leave,' she says.

I can feel her anger now in a way that I couldn't before I left for Bristol.

As we sit, I know that I have to say the thing that I've probably known all along, but can only understand now.

'The thing is,' I say, 'after Mum died I only thought about myself. I just couldn't deal with any of it so in the end I ran away. I honestly had no idea what else to do.'

'I know,' she says, 'but you hurt me.'

'I know I did,' I say, 'and I'm so sorry. I wish I hadn't. After Mum died, I felt completely numb. I should have seen that it wasn't like that for you, but I couldn't see past myself.'

I can feel tears in my eyes. 'I'm really sorry,' I say.

She puts her hand on mine.

'I know,' she says, softly.

We sit with one hand holding our mugs and the other each other's. There's more stuff that we both want to say, but it's not ready to come out, not right now anyway.

'Will you go back to Bristol?' she asks after a while.

'I'm not sure,' I say. 'It depends.'

'On what?'

'Lots of things. I mean, for one thing, I'm not sure I'd be able, definitely not at the moment,' I say.

'What do you mean? Why not?'

'I couldn't live on my own.'

'But you don't seem that bad.'

'I know. I speak all right so people think I *am* all right. "A good facade," they called it in the hospital. They said I'd have to be careful as people won't understand what's happened. There's a lot of problems, really.'

'Oh,' she says, and we don't speak again for a bit.

'What was it like in the hospital?' she asks.

'Well, I don't remember a lot of it, but it was all right, I think. The nurses were really nice.'

'Oh yeah?'

'Not like that,' I say, laughing. 'Just really kind, sort of pure. It might sound strange but I felt really safe, like I used to feel with my mum when I was really little.'

'That's nice, I'm glad,' she says, and squeezes my hand.

We talk about Bristol, the cardiac arrest and the brain injury, and her parents and my mum, and what she's been doing.

'So, you finished at Falmouth? You're not going to carry on?' I ask.

'Well, I finished the Art Foundation when you were in Bristol, but I didn't see the point in carrying on and doing a full degree. I want to make my jewellery and I don't need a degree for that.'

'Were your parents all right with it?'

'Yeah, fine. I mean, Mum only did a Foundation and look at her.'

Sophie's mum, Pam, is a ceramicist, and she makes sculptures and really intricate vases and stuff. Sophie calls her Mrs Potter to tease her. And it is true that a lot of the time her mum was at her potter's wheel in her studio on the side of their house. More often than not when I was there she had clay all up her arms.

'My jewellery's good, you know. People are buying it.'

'I know it is,' I say. 'It's really good.'

We carry on talking like this and then I realise I'd better get going back to Jacob.

'How is Jacob?' she asks as I'm leaving.

'He's all right,' I say. 'Do you want to come up to see him at the farm?'

'I will,' Sophie says. 'Soon.'

Back in the Guildhall, the farmers' market is still going strong. There's a man playing guitar with a small amp in the corner and a lot of people milling about. The noise goes right through me and I feel disorientated and dizzy. I go up to Jacob. He's sold most of his things.

'Hello,' he says while handing change to a customer with a basket full of vegetables. 'I'll be finishing up in a bit. Half an hour, I'll be done. Will you bring the cart down?'

'Will do,' I say, turning to leave.

'Did you go to Calico's?'

'Oh no, I forgot. Sorry. I'll go now on the way to the cart.'

I like hardware shops and Calico's is a proper one, every inch of the walls covered with everything you could ever imagine needing, with mop heads and washing lines and packs of pegs dangling from the ceiling, buckets bursting with plungers and rubber mallets. I ask for the screws on my list, and the man weighs them out on the same sort of scales they used to have in sweet shops with a dull brass balloon-shaped bowl on one side and a tray for the little brass weights on the other. It smells nice in here too, of metal and wood chips. I also buy a little block of balsa wood and a scalpel as I've the idea of carving something for Jacob. I used to be quite good at carving and hopefully I still am since the brain injury.

As I head back up the hill, my mind returns to Roger Minack. His warning has had the opposite effect to what he intended. Or maybe this is what he intended – to stir me up so much that I couldn't not try to find out what Bill Sligo is up to. Either way, it doesn't matter, as now it's even more important that I find out. If Sligo wants Jacob's field for something illegal and might be willing to hurt Jacob to make him sell it, I can go to the police and they will put a stop to it. Sligo wouldn't even need to know it was me who had gone to the police; it could be an anonymous tip. Only, just now, I have no idea how I can possibly find out what he's doing. When was it that that lawyer's letter arrived? I'm hopeless at measuring time now, but it must have been more than a month ago, so the deadline has been and gone. But no word from Sligo, or not as far as I know. I wonder whether Sligo will up his offer or try to force Jacob's hand another way? My stomach tightens with the thought and old anxieties that I thought had died with the cardiac arrest come rushing back.

On the road back to the farm, I ask Jacob before I can stop myself, 'Did you reply to that letter from the solicitors?'

I feel straight away that I shouldn't have raised it, but still I can't let it lie, the hard ball in my stomach pushing the words up and out. 'You're not worried about what he'll do when he doesn't get what he wants?'

'Worried?' Jacob says, smiling. 'No, I am not. And nor should you be.' He looks over at me now and I know he can see the worry all over my face. 'That man ain't getting his hands on that field or any other field of ours for that matter.' He turns his gaze back to the road and adds, 'And that's that,' and I know that what he's really saying is that he won't talk about it again, and I already know that I won't ask him again either.

Field of ours, I think as we sway slightly from side to side on the cart, like it's our farm, a family farm. I like this, and for a while it washes away my uneasiness and I just sit in the quiet watching the hedgerows and occasional glimpses of fields to the left and the sea to the right. *That field of ours.*

12

'Was it good takings, then?' I ask as we're unloading the small amount of leftover stuff from the cart. Most of it was sold, including all of Granny Carne's jars, which I am happy about.

'Not bad,' Jacob says, 'not bad at all. Should keep the wolf from the door for a while at least.' He laughs, and I laugh too but I don't feel like it, not at all. The mention of the wolf at the door has sent my mind straight back to Bill Sligo and I imagine him prowling around the farm, coming closer and closer to the farmhouse.

'What are you brooding about?' Jacob asks, pulling me out of my thoughts.

'Oh, not brooding, just a bit tired.'

'Well, no wonder, it's been a long day. Curry tonight and an early bed.'

'Oh, nice,' I say, 'did you get a sauce?'

There's a woman who sells homemade curry sauce at the market – Ruby Murray's – and they're really good.

'I did. And naan and mango chutney, so we're set.'

'Great,' I say and my stomach rumbles as I remember that I forgot to have any lunch. I won't tell Jacob this, though, as he knows how I often forget to eat if he hasn't sorted something, and then he feels bad about it.

'I saw Sophie in St Ives,' I say when we sit down to eat.

'Oh yes?'

'Yeah, I passed the bookshop and she came out. She said she wrote to you.'

'That she did.'

'And she asked you not to tell me.'

'That's right.'

'She said it was because she wanted to see me when she saw me.'

'Yes, that's what she said in her letter. Well, I can see her point. It's a big thing that happened to you, and you hear all sorts of things about people with brain injuries. Changed personalities, all sorts. I imagine she was nervous.'

'I haven't changed, have I?'

'Not like that, no. She's written a number of times, mind. And I've written back. Eat up, your food's going cold.'

I have a couple of forkfuls.

'What about?' I say.

'Asking after you, of course.'

'She could have just come down here to see me.'

'Well, she could. As I say, I expect she was nervous and wanted to give you time.'

'Maybe,' I say.

Jacob puts down his knife and fork and looks at me. 'Would you like to know what I think?'

'Go on then,' I say.

'Let the past be in the past.'

'You mean I shouldn't see her again?'

'No, that's not what I mean. What I mean is you and

Sophie have a past. Just don't let that past stand in the way of anything.'

I am so tired I go straight to bed after dinner. Usually I'd be asleep as soon as my head hits the pillow, but I lie thinking about Sophie. I try to picture her and her face flashes in my mind's eye and then it's gone just as quickly. But I can sort of feel what it was to be close to her, and the feeling is stronger than any visual memory ever could be.

   The thing is, we didn't split up because we didn't like each other any more, or we got on each other's nerves or anything like that. It was just a funny time, a strange time. After my mum died I was sort of in my own world. I remember the day after the night she died I went out to get some coffee. I was looking at all the people around whose mums hadn't just died and I felt so separate from them, like they were on one side of a pane of glass and I was on the other. Maybe that's what happens when you are with someone when they're dying. You go as far as you can into the world of the dead with them and then once they've died it takes a while to come back.

   Well, I think it took me a long time. Sophie would say things like how distant I was. I'd feel bad, but I didn't know how to be any different. It was that that split us up really. I didn't love her any less and I don't think she stopped loving me. I sort of disappeared into myself. Going to Bristol was just living out what was going on in my head, separating myself from everything and everyone. I think maybe I thought that if I wasn't in St Ives, not with Sophie, and not around anyone else I knew, it could be like Mum hadn't died at all. I've never thought of it like this before, but now that

I have, I'm sure I'm right. And it worked a bit. Of course I didn't forget Mum was dead, but in Bristol I didn't have to look at it, not directly. I didn't tell a single person there that she had died. I was trying to make it like it had never happened, but of course I didn't realise that at the time.

I missed Sophie so much, but it was easier not being with her because she made me think so much of Mum, not because they were similar, but because they were the two people I loved most in the world, so when Mum was gone, being with Sophie just made me feel it even more. Now it seems so stupid, to have walked away from Sophie as if that might change what had happened. I think grief made me go a bit mad, and I didn't know how to undo what I had done.

We weren't really friends before we got together, me and Sophie. We hung out together in the same big group, surfing or having bonfires on the beach, and we had a laugh but we didn't really know each other. We hadn't been to the same secondary school. After primary in St Ives, Sophie went to the private girls' school in Truro and I went to the comp here. Her parents are quite well off. Her dad is a partner in a granite quarry and her mum's pretty well known now and sells loads of work and has shows and stuff.

Their house is really nice. It's right in the middle of St Ives but you wouldn't know because it's surrounded by a high stone wall. Sophie's mum loves gardening and inside the wall she has all sorts of tropical plants that only grow down here in Cornwall.

Not that you would know that they have money from meeting them. They're not at all flashy, and their house is normal. Much bigger than mine and Mum's cottage was, but not mad big, and just nice inside. Homely with art all over the place. And they were so nice to me when Mum died. I mostly stayed with them up until I went to Bristol as I really didn't want to be in the cottage on my own. I don't think they were angry when me and Sophie split up. I think they just thought it was really sad.

But anyway, before all that, Sophie and I knew each other from the beach, but that was it really. Most people growing up in St Ives know each other a bit and hang out on the beach or around the harbour.

Me and my mates hung around with a lot of girls, but Sophie was nothing like the rest. She was self-contained and never looked for attention or played up to things. She just sort of kept her course no matter what anyone else was doing. She also didn't speak for the sake of it, and I really liked that. It made her all the more mysterious.

She's also absolutely beautiful and nothing like the other girls to look at. She's quite tall and slim, but strong and solid like she's really grounded. I fancied her for sure, but then there was this moment when I properly fell for her. We were all on the beach, at the far end near Man's Head. It used to be that only locals hung out there. The sun was setting and we all went in the water. When we came out again, she stood there in the shallows, her dark wavy hair dripping wet. And she was covered in goosebumps all over her dark brown skin and her nipples were showing through her bikini. I could hardly breathe and I was trembling all over.

After that I thought about her all the time. I'd try to get her on her own to talk to on the beach. And all the time I was so worried that someone else would come in and get her attention and I would lose her. But all the other guys were more interested in the girls who were trying to look the same as each other and who flirted in a way that seemed so obvious. I felt like I had discovered this precious thing that everyone else had overlooked. That's what eventually gave me the courage to kiss her for the first time. I had been thinking about how to do it for what felt like ages, but I kept bottling it. In the end I told my mum about it and she told me to get on with it. 'She won't wait around for ever,' she said, and that was enough to scare me into doing it.

We always made fires with driftwood on nice evenings, and we were all sitting around the bonfire one evening when I asked her really quietly if she wanted to walk down on the beach so the others wouldn't hear. She stood up and we walked along the beach, me with my arm around her. I can't remember what we were talking about. My heart was beating so hard, I couldn't really concentrate.

When we got the end of the beach we climbed up to this bit on the rocks that's totally hidden away. It was just us, the sky and the sea. We sat down and I leaned in as smoothly as I could, trying not to be awkward. Then she kissed me back and it was wild. I'd kissed other girls, but it had never been like that.

We did a lot of kissing and other stuff over the next few weeks, and then one day she asked me if I wanted to stay over. She'd even asked her mum if it was OK, and her mum said it was, so long as my mum didn't mind. It didn't bother me asking Mum as I was always really open with her, so it wasn't embarrassing. When I asked her, she said it was fine as long as I wasn't going to break Sophie's heart and as long as I was sure. Well, I wasn't going to do that, and I was definitely sure.

That was it after that night. I was addicted to Sophie, and she was the same with me. We did it everywhere, at any time. We often went back to that place on the rocks and did it there late in the evening when no one was around. Although, one time we did get caught. We were in our usual spot on the rock when this woman saw us. The rocks there kind of merge into the cliff path above, and she had scrambled down after her dog when she spotted us.

'I can see your bottom, young man. You should be ashamed!'

Well, I wasn't ashamed but I was definitely embarrassed. Sophie wasn't, though. She thought the whole thing was hilarious. After that, every now and then when she saw me naked from behind, she'd shout 'I can see your bottom, young man' and laugh her head off.

This is the thing about Sophie. She really, really doesn't care what other people think of her. She's a very kind person and she thinks that so long as you are kind to other people, you don't need to worry about anything else. People might like you or might try to make you feel bad about yourself for whatever reason, but that was their business, she thought. I really liked that about her, but not just that. I liked everything about her. When we got together we talked and talked. I soaked up anything she said and I learned something new about her each time – the way she sipped her tea, holding the mug with both hands, or how much she liked reading mystery novels and how she loved nature and worried about it – until I knew her better than anyone else in the world and she knew me the best too.

Seeing her today was so strange. All my feelings for her are still there. They haven't changed at all, but they're just out of reach. It's this apathy thing. Every feeling I have is so blunt it makes me want to cry sometimes, only I can't because my emotions aren't strong enough. Or they are strong enough, but they're just out of touching distance. Yes, that's it. It was the same when I held her hand today. That would have sent an electric shock though me before. Today, I felt something but nothing like before. I feel like I can live with all the other problems, but this is like part of me has died.

I just hope it hasn't. I hope it's only sleeping.

13

When I wake it is dark, but light is coming through the open door, and Jacob is shaking my leg and saying something to me. Someone is falling, he's saying.

'What? Who?'

'Niamh. The foal. It's coming.'

'Oh, right,' I say, clambering out of bed, unsteady on my feet as my brain catches up with the sudden movement. You wouldn't normally have a horse foaling in November. They normally come in the spring, but Niamh got pregnant late last year. It wasn't deliberate, Jacob's not the sort who tries to control a horse's cycle, to manipulate it. He thought it might have been the Indian summer last year that tricked her body into ovulating so late, or just a fluke perhaps. It's not a problem; it just means we have to make sure the foal is warm enough in the stable and we've been packing it with extra straw for a few weeks now, ready for the arrival.

'Now, we shouldn't have to do anything at all,' Jacob says in the kitchen. 'We'll be there just in case.'

We've already been through this many times, but Jacob is nervous: I can feel it as I've felt it before when he's been talking about the upcoming birth. He knows what he's doing all right. It's just a risky time for the mare and the foal, especially with the colder weather. As well as the extra straw, there's a wood burner in the stable, in the corner, well away from the straw and behind a metal fire guard like the one we had at home over the fireplace when I was little.

The other worry is that if something went wrong with the birth we don't have a telephone to call the vet, but Jacob's already said that if something does happen, I'm to ride to Mrs Beaton's and use her phone. I've had the vet's number on a piece of paper in my jeans pocket, in the little square for coins, for a while.

'And we need to be very quiet and slow in our movements. Niamh trusts us, so she won't mind us being there, but still, we've got to respect her space.'

'I will,' I say.

'Good lad.'

He picks up a hurricane lamp from the windowsill, lights it and we head outside. There's a chill in the air and I can see my breath billow out in the lamplight, but it's more damp than really cold.

An amber glow comes from the flicker of the fire.

'Here we are,' Jacob says softly as we go in. 'How's it going, old girl?'

Niamh's standing in the corner of the stable, her belly bulging with the unborn foal. Jacob approaches her and strokes her nose. It's completely quiet in here. Connor is in the barn with the cows, so the only sounds are those of the three of us breathing and the occasional rustle of our feet in the straw. Niamh's eyes shine in the lamplight; her gaze is soft as if her attention has turned inwards and her surroundings hold no interest for her.

Jacob looks at her underside. 'Won't be long now,' he

says. 'Colostrum, see?' He beckons me to come forward and I see a bead of milky fluid shining on the end of her teat. Jacob told me about this. It's full of all the antibodies the foal will need to get it started. Jacob goes round behind her and puts his arm up her.

'Yep,' he says, 'that's fine, not far off now.' Jacob looks more relaxed, like Niamh's calm has passed into him. I feel it too, and I think of the dream or vision I had months ago in the hospital of the Irish nurses and their lilting whispers.

Niamh moans and all of a sudden she's foaling. It happens so quickly, and all Jacob has to do is stand behind her and gently ease the foal out of her. It slides from her like water from the pump and lands in the straw. Straight away, it thrashes around as if trying to make sense of its body, to work out what to do.

'What a beauty,' Jacob says. 'Look at that, old girl. Look at those colourings,' he adds, turning to me.

The foal's legs are brown with long white socks up to the knees. They are very long and gangly, out of proportion, the way babies' heads look too big for their bodies.

'Isn't she a beauty?' Jacob says to himself more than to me. He heaps straw around the squirming body but the foal's already trying to make her way over to suckle her mother. She shifts her body in lurching movements, rising up and launching herself forwards.

'Oh!' I say as she dives headfirst into the straw.

'She's fine, don't worry,' Jacob says. 'She'll be on her feet in no time, this one.'

Niamh turns her head to the side and looks at the foal for a moment; then she looks fowards again.

'That's right, there she is,' Jacob says. 'You done good, Niamh.'

Behind her the afterbirth shimmers in the soft light.

'Why don't you give her a hand and help her up,' Jacob says, looking at me. 'Here.' He stands behind the foal and slides his hand under her belly, lifting her slightly, and beckons to me to do the same. I step forward and put my hands where Jacob's are. The foal is beautifully warm and soft. Already she feels strong, her body firm and pulsing with energy.

'That's the way,' Jacob says, 'let's get her around here a bit so Niamh can see her.' Gently we help the foal so she's half lying, half raised up on the knees of her forelegs in front of her mother. We retreat to the furthest corner and watch as Niamh lowers her head and begins to lick and nuzzle her foal, who lifts her head up to meet her mother's.

'Perfect,' Jacob says. 'They'll get on just fine.'

We sit down on the straw, side by side, legs stretched out in front of us, backs leaning up against the wall, and we watch. The only sounds are the soft rustle of the horses and our own breath. My chest rises and falls slightly quicker than Jacob's long deep breaths which are like the pistons of a huge machine. The flames in the wood burner are low now, rolling over the embers that ripple and glow red like jewels flashing.

'What should we call her?' Jacob asks in a whisper.

'Ruby,' I say without even thinking.

'Ruby,' says Jacob, and it's settled.

14

I spend my days with Ruby. It's amazing seeing her grow. I wonder whether babies grow this quickly. I've started grooming her, which is really important to make a bond. First I groom Niamh so Ruby can see it's nothing to worry about, then I go to her. Ruby's really good with it already and I think she likes it. And the days and weeks slip by with grooming, and taking Connor out. I've also started carving something for Jacob out of that block of balsa wood I bought in the hardware shop. It's a little carving of Niamh with her harness on. I'm just doing little bits each day as it takes quite a lot of concentration.

All this time I don't forget about Bill Sligo. If anything, he occupies my mind more and more like a drop of ink spreading its tendrils through water. The thought of him sits in my head and in my stomach, pulling me off centre, off balance. I lie in bed imagining encountering him on the track, confronting him, fighting him, even though I've never had a fight in my life. I bet he's had loads. In my imagination I beat him, though, and tell him not to show his face around here again and I know he won't. He submits like a dog that knows the fight is lost. Then I come back to reality and my stomach lurches.

I concoct plans to find out more about him. I think about

trying to get hold of his criminal record, but really there's no way I'd be able to. Then I think about following him, but how could I without a car? I could go back to his house and try to eavesdrop, but it would be too risky.

These same thoughts and ideas circle in my head like the horses on a merry-go-round, each one right in front of me, then disappearing only to return unchanged. Ruminating, I think it's called. So, I ruminate and ruminate, nothing changing, making no progress.

The deadline for Jacob to accept the offer in Sligo's solicitor's letter has long been and gone. For a while I was expecting him to turn up demanding that Jacob sell him the field. I imagined him wild, his black eyes flashing. But there was nothing and no sign of him.

I've been with the horses all day today, and when I come back in the first thing I see is a letter propped up against a mug on the table, addressed to me. I know it is from Sophie. I'd recognise her writing anywhere. It's very artistic but also very neat. She can write with her hand completely off the paper because she was given handwriting lessons for years when she was growing up as her mum thought it was so important. I love her writing, especially compared to mine.

We wrote to each other all the time when we were going out. Letters, or little notes, but especially postcards. Sophie liked those old-fashioned ones with drawings of caricature people on the beach and little innuendoes written by them. We would try to outdo each other with the best card we could each find.

I take the letter and go to the armchair. Even though it's just a short note I find myself reading it over and over again. She says she'll come to visit on Saturday unless I write to say not to.

I do want her to come. A lot. I feel the closest I've felt to excitement since before the brain injury. I fold the letter and put it in my pocket.

15

It's cold now. Jacob says the jet stream has shifted. I don't know how he knows this. He reads the sky like other people read the weather forecast in the newspaper.

'It'll be harsh this winter. Storms too,' he said yesterday. Every day we pack the stable and the barn with straw. They get through bales and bales of it, the horses and the cows. I like pulling the bales apart; the smell that bursts out of them reminds me of the late-summer days as if the sunshine was rolled up with the straw.

On the coldest days, when the wind races over the farm from the sea, bitter and raw, we put rugs on the horses so they can still be out in the fields. And at night, Jacob keeps the wood burner going in the stable for Ruby.

'Just 'til she's a little stronger,' he says, although she already seems very strong to me, gambolling away from Niamh and then coming back to her like a child testing the boundaries but still wanting to stay close. I worry about the wood burner, that a fire could start and then what? We have no telephone. When I say this to Jacob, he chuckles.

'Decades there's been a fire burning in there and no bother. Fire's no harm so long as you respect it.'

Now when the worry rises up in me, I think of the fire

guard and how Jacob keeps the floor around the fire swept clear of the straw.

It's been quite a good day today. Not too tired, headache OK. That meant I didn't have a rest so I'm tired now, very. We've had our dinner, cottage pie with the mash fluffed up on top with cheese mixed in so it went golden brown in the oven. Peas, too, which are the only greens I eat. And Bisto gravy. I'm full and sleepy, sitting on my window seat to look at the sky for a minute before I go to bed. It's a totally clear night, the moon a half-crescent and as white and bright as snow. My left optic nerve was damaged during the cardiac arrest, so my sight is fuzzy in that eye, but if I cover it I can see the stars quite clearly with my right, millions of them, light years away. I can't get my head around that. You'd think that the light would fizzle out on its way here, run out of steam, but there they are, pricks of ancient light piercing the endless darkness.

I'll go to sleep once I've seen a shooting star. You just have to wait long enough. One time, when I was eleven or maybe twelve, me and my friend Tom slept on the beach, staring up at the sky and counting shooting stars. There were so many, so many more than you'd think. We'd scan the sky and then call out with pure excitement when we saw one. It's harder for me to see them now with my visual problems. I'm hoping one falls right in the middle of my field of vision.

My eyes are starting to ache from straining so I shift my gaze down to the ground to rest them before having another go. Then I see something. Another light, but at ground level, and it's moving, bobbing up and down a little. I can't think what it is, but as I watch I realise that it's a torch, or someone holding a torch and walking along the track, down towards the bottom field. My heartbeat rises into my throat. I can't see anything other than the bobbing light, but it's Bill Sligo, I'm sure of it.

I know straight away that I'm going to follow him. I'm on my feet, pulling on my jeans and my thick jumper. I take my own torch from my bedside table and push the end of it into my pocket. I know that Jacob would stop me if he knew what I was doing, so I slide my feet over the floorboards so as not to step too heavily on the creaking ones. Halfway across the room, halfway to the door, I feel a board give under my foot and know that it will cry out when I release my weight. I pause, stock still. The farmhouse is silent but for the muffled rumble of Jacob's snores, like distant thunder. I have no choice. That light will be disappearing down the path. I glance back at the window and already I can't see it. I lift my foot, and the sound of the floorboard fills the room. Better now to get out quickly and make all my noise in one go rather than string it out. I hurry to the door on tiptoes and take the stairs softly but quickly.

In the kitchen, moonlight shines through the window and stretches over the flagstones. At the door, I put on my heavy coat and my boots and very slowly cover half the latch mechanism with my left hand and slide the bolt open with my right. Jacob's the sort of person who regularly greases bolts and hinges, so it glides open with a pleasing swish. I lift the latch in the same careful way, listening out one more time for Jacob, and then I'm outside.

The air is sharp in my throat and lungs. I can just make out my breath in the moonlight, which makes the pebbled path in front of me glow like dimpled snow. I step on to the thick tufts of grass to the side of the path to avoid crunching, then I'm safely on the stone cobbles of the yard. The air around me is dense with the night's silence, and through it, as if amplified, comes a soft shuffle of the horses shifting position in the stable. I walk quickly over the yard, through the gate, on to the track, and then I run. I keep to the grass in the middle of the lane between the tyre tracks. It's crisp with frost and the ground beneath it is on the way to being frozen, but it's quiet enough. I'll jog just for a bit to catch up and then I'll walk. That way he won't hear me behind him. I stick to the left-hand side, in the shadows of the hedgerows. On the other side, the frosty leaves shimmer in the moonlight.

I only jog for a short time before I think better of it. First there's the noise of my breath stopping me from hearing properly, but mainly I can't see so well in the dark these days. The shadows are deep inky wells and, with no contours, the ground is an abyss. I walk on as quickly as I dare, my arms held out in front of me, groping the dark. I'm guided by the silvery bushes to my right and the tufts of grass below my feet. I know that apart from a stray bramble I won't walk into anything. I can't see Bill Sligo's torchlight, or hear anything. I stop now and then to listen, straining to hear the sound of boots scuffing the track. Maybe he too is keeping to the grass?

My balance is not good in the dark: I keep stumbling and then stopping to listen. Have I been heard? I don't think so. I don't feel nervous or afraid, though. My heart isn't pounding; my breath is smooth and even. This is part of the apathy, not caring about the consequences of what I am doing. I'm not sure whether this is a good thing or a bad thing.

I am at the end of the track now. The bushes fall away

from my sides and the field opens up, sloping away from me down to the sea, which is cut clean in half by a diamond-bright blade of moonlight.

Down by the wheelhouse is the silhouette of a figure and a pool of torchlight. I walk faster now. I don't fear detection as he wouldn't see me if he turned around. I wouldn't be outlined by the moonlight the way he is. He's alone, and right beside the wheelhouse now. I stop and kneel down, my gaze fixed on him, afraid that if I look away I won't find him again. I hear rustling in the grass to my left. Field mice or a hedgehog perhaps. I've looked away, got distracted, and as I look back to the place there is no light other than the moon on the sea. Where has he gone? I think for a moment that he's gone down the cliff but you would be mad to do that. The rock face is almost sheer here, which is why we had to replace the fence straight away. I stand up again and start to creep down towards the wheelhouse, its hulking silhouette seeming to float on the steely water beyond.

The torch comes on again, and I stop, going straight to ground. He's in the shadow of the wheelhouse and I'm closer to him than I want to be, but I daren't move again now I know he's only a stone's throw away. He's no longer pointing his torch at the ground. There's no pool of light at his feet. Instead he's pointing it out to sea. I'm at an angle to him and I can see a sliver of light from the side of the torch, flashing on and off. It comes on in bursts. One, two, three, pause. One, two, three, pause. Then nothing and the black night takes over again, and I wonder: Did I really see that, or was it some sort of visual dysfunction thing?

But then another flicker towards the edge of my peripheral

vision draws my eyes towards it. Another light: one, two, three, pause; one, two, three. This light is out on the sea, but close in to the cliffs, dangerously close if it was rough, but there's only the slightest sound of the swell on the rocks below.

And now a noise. The engine of a boat starts up. For a moment it gets louder and I think it is heading straight for the cliffs, but it must have turned because now it's growing fainter. I stay in my spot, crouched down, the grass cold and damp on my hands and knees. I watch Bill Sligo's silhouette, standing still as a statue. Then he turns towards me, towards the track back up the field, and suddenly his face looms out of the dark, lit by the flame of a cigarette lighter cupped in his hands, a ghost floating with no body. He starts to walk back towards me, and I have nowhere to go. If I run he might well catch me. I hunch down, my body compact and my face turned down to the ground so the moon doesn't catch it. I hold my breath.

His feet swoosh over the grass and I hear his breathing and the muffled popping sound as he inhales smoke from his cigarette. I smell that, too, strongly. My face is so close to the ground that the grass prickles on my lips. What am I going to do if he sees me? I mustn't think about that now. I focus on my heart beating in my chest and I'm surprised it isn't faster, and again I realise I'm not afraid. What will be will be. For a moment I think I'll stand, confront him, ask him what he thinks he's doing on Jacob's land. Then, as quickly as the idea comes, I realise how stupid that would be, so I stay down, still holding my breath as he passes me and makes his way up the field. I stay motionless, holding my breath.

When I can't hear him any more, I breathe out and lift my

head cautiously. There's no sign of Sligo, but the cold air is still laced with the smell of burnt tobacco. It smells rank, as I imagine he smells too.

He's gone now. The pool of light from his torch is bobbing away up the hill. I stand. At first I stagger, dizzy and disorientated in the dark; then I steady myself and begin to walk down the slope towards the mineshaft. I look out to sea, straining for sight of the boat, but beyond the glimmering slash of moonlight on the water, there's nothing but an endless darkness that seems to fill my head as I stare into it. No sound either, other than the gentle heaving swell on the rocks below.

There's nothing around the mine, and when I pull myself up and shine my torch on to the trap door, it's still locked.

On the way back up to the farm, I go through the things I know.

One. Bill Sligo is a criminal. He killed Granny Carne's nephew, and according to Betty up at Hawthorn Farm, he's a drug dealer too.

Two. I search my mind for the second thing but my train of thought has gone like a candle just blown out. I try to think but all I get is this static fuzz of a 3 a.m. TV screen. Suddenly, I desperately need to sleep and I quicken my pace up the track.

At the farm, I let myself in quietly, sliding the bolts back across the door very carefully. Then I creep upstairs and collapse on to my bed.

16

I wake and I'm thirsty, still in my jeans and jumper. It's almost midday. I wonder whether Jacob came in and saw me fully dressed. If he did, I'll just have to say I was so tired I fell asleep before getting ready for bed. I go over to the sink, drink a large glass of cold fresh water, then another, undress, wash quickly and get back into bed, trying to remember exactly what happened last night. There was Sligo and the boat and the signalling with the torch. I close my eyes and try to picture it but nothing comes. I try to see his silhouette, but again nothing. So what was he doing there and who was he signalling to? I try to think of all the things I know and to put them in some sort of order. I can't get past two without losing track of where I am, so I take out my notebook and start a list.

1. *Sligo was out in the middle of the night, on Jacob's land, signalling to a boat.*
2. *Sligo killed Granny Carne's Cadan. He's also a drug dealer according to Betty at Hawthorn Farm.*
3. *He's got loads of dodgy mates and one of them tried to run me and Connor off the road.*
4. *He wants to buy Jacob's field and was in a hurry to do it, and was willing to pay more than it is worth.*

The last point gets me thinking about that field. Why does he want that particular field? What's special about it? Then it hits me and it's so obvious. The wheelhouse. He was signalling from the wheelhouse. But it's not like he was showing the boat where to land. The nearest place to moor a boat is St Ives harbour. Any boat would be wrecked on the rocks if they came in too close, and anyway, even if they could come in, there's the cliff. Could it just be a signal for the boat to get its bearings? No, thousands of ships and boats sail these waters without that. It must be the mine*shaft* he's interested in. Maybe it has an exit further down the cliff, by the sea. Then I remember the other thing – number 5 for the list. The new cover over the mine.

I look over the list again and it all seems obvious now. Bill Sligo wants to bring drugs off the boat and up the mineshaft. He wants to fill the gap left by that gang we read about in the *Echo*. It's a good plan. Who would ever know? Except he doesn't want Jacob or probably me anywhere near it so he wants the field and the mine shaft for himself.

I want to get a look at the wheelhouse and the cliff below from the sea and I know just how to do it. I look at the clock again. If I leave now I can be in St Ives in an hour and Jacob won't even notice as he'll be out in the fields somewhere. I feel bad for not helping him, but then remind myself that he doesn't really want me helping him anyway. He wants me resting. I'm not doing that either, of course, but I am trying to help him. I'll drop into the bookshop too.

I get dressed again, put my hat, scarf, binoculars and a notebook in my backpack and head downstairs where there's some cold toast and coffee on the side and I have them both, pushing an apple into the pocket of my jacket before heading out.

I see the top of the bus from Penzance coming over the lip of the hill as I get to the top of the lane, and I run the last two hundred metres or so, my chest still aching from the operation and the heavy breathing from the short run setting off the pain. I used to be so fit.

I like this bus. It's the open-top tourist bus, and me and Mum used to take it every now and then just for fun.

'All right,' I say to the driver.

'All right,' he says, nodding to me.

I recognise him. He also drives this seasonal bus heaving with sunburnt holidaymakers from Porthmeor Beach up to the rugby-club car park, willing the battered old thing up the steep hill by Barnoon Cemetery.

It's almost empty on the bus and I take the front seat at the top, which is the best seat obviously, except when you're a teenager and then the back seat is the best. The view stretches all the way to Godrevy Lighthouse, which is the one in Virginia Woolf's book *To the Lighthouse* that Granny Carne has.

It's clear today, and still. A good day to go out on a boat. Which is what I'm planning to do. There are boat trips from the harbour to the Carracks, or Seal Island as the tour operators call it on their posters. It's a tiny outcrop of rocks, just off the cliffs, where there's a small colony of seals. Nothing like the huge colony at Godrevy Head where you often can't see the beach below for the mass of writhing seals.

Anyway, the point is that the Carracks are just down the coast from us, so the seal-trip boats pass us on the way there.

With my binoculars, I should be able to see the base of the cliff below the mineshaft clearly from the boat. I just hope the boats are still running as it's December now and they don't always run in low season, especially if the sea's up, but there's been no real wind for a while now.

As I get off the bus and walk down the Stennack, I have a vivid flash of a memory of walking up here one evening in the pouring rain, water running down the hill in ladders. That's what my mum said anyway, and it did look like ladders, or rope ladders perhaps, the steps bowed.

Down, past the old post office, past the cinema, the hardware shop, the library, Tregenna Place, the church, and out into the harbour. The Christmas lights are up but not yet lit. It's very quiet. This is how I like it. I can't take crowds any more. There are a few people milling about, including a couple holding ice creams even though it's quite cold. And yes, there it is. The boat-trip stand with two men chatting to each other and smoking.

'All right,' I say.

'All right.'

'You going out today?' I ask them.

'Can do. If you like.' He's not being rude. This is just how these guys are.

'To the Carracks?'

'Can do. Mackerel, or just the trip?'

'Just the trip,' I say, then I think again. If I could take back some mackerel then I'd have a good reason for having come into town.

'Actually, mackerel, if that's all right.'

'All right. Give us twenty minutes, see if anyone else

wants to join,' he says before shouting to an almost empty quay, 'Mackerel fishing! Guaranteed catch! Anyone for mackerel?'

'Just going to get a coffee. I'll be back in a minute. Want one?' I ask him. He doesn't, but he seems pleased to have been asked. I wander down to the place that used to be the Wimpy. I remember a flood here too, late one summer evening, with water filling up the floor of the Wimpy. I drink my espresso at the counter and walk back out to the boat stand.

There's a man there now with a young boy, six or seven maybe, something like that. The man is tall with neat hair. He has a face that looks like it's never really very relaxed. The boy looks happier. Carefree, enjoying his day with his dad.

'Is this us then?' the skipper asks.

'Yep, that's it,' the other one answers.

'Come on then.'

We walk round the harbour to Smeaton's Pier, down the granite steps and on to the boat. It's a small one. Room for eight or so, plenty of room with just the three of us. The skipper and his mate are in the little wheelhouse. His mate comes out and slings a life jacket to each of us, and then we're off, slowly at first as we leave the harbour, then he opens up the throttle and the bow lifts, and the three of us slide back along the benches. The boy is thrilled with this. He doesn't say anything but he gives his dad a look that would say 'Phwoooor' if this was drawn in a comic book. There's a tinge of sadness as I watch this, knowing the feeling of excitement the boy has now, but no longer being able to access it myself.

'Not at this stage,' the doctor had said last time I asked whether the apathy symptoms would improve.

It's only safe to let feelings in a little at a time, drip by drip, otherwise they would overwhelm me, I think.

I smile at the boy and his dad when they look over to me, not wanting to dampen the moment with an expressionless face, even though I'm not sad.

'Birds or boats?' the man says to me, and I look at him trying to process what he is saying.

'Binoculars,' he says, nodding at them hanging around my neck.

'Oh,' I say, 'sorry, bit slow. Birds, mainly.'

'Is it true there are puffins?'

'Can be,' I say, 'but not at this time of year. Spring and summer months.'

'Ah.' He turns away, looking a bit disheartened.

'Might possibly see a guillemot, though, if we're lucky. Jet black with feet as red as Father Christmas's coat,' I say, mostly to the boy. He seems to like the idea of that. 'And I'm sure we'll see a few seals out by the Carracks.'

'That would be good, wouldn't it?' the dad says to the boy.

'I'm Mike,' he says to me. 'And this is Tom.'

'Jago.'

'You visiting, or . . .'

'No, I live here. Just up there actually.' I point to the land in the direction of the farm. 'Where are you from?'

'Warwick.'

'Long way,' I say.

'Not bad on the train.'

The boy points to a tanker on the horizon and I'm relieved

that the conversation ended at the juncture where I either have to go into what happened to me or end up being vague and probably coming across rude. I look to shore. Porthmeor Beach is quiet. It's best like that, I think. Past Man's Head now. There's more swell out here, enough to need to hold on to the rail along the side of the boat. The boy is chattering to his dad about something but I can't hear him over the engine. I watch a couple of walkers on the coast path, probably heading to Zennor and the Tinners Arms, and my mind goes to Granny Carne's nephew being killed off Zennor Head by Bill Sligo.

There's not much to see in the way of birds, not that I'm really bothered today. We've slowed down now and I hear the boy asking when we are doing the fishing.

'Not sure,' the dad says, looking at me.

'It'll be on the way back,' I say. 'We'll come in on the current near St Ives and fish then.'

Our wheelhouse is coming into view now. It's smaller from this aspect, compact and hunched into the landscape. Holding the binoculars as steady as I can, I follow a straight line down the cliff face to the sea, and I see it straight away. A triangular opening in the rocks and, at the base of it, above sea level, a sort of platform at the entrance, hewn into the rock. It must lead into the mineshaft, surely, and from there up to the wheelhouse. At high tide that platform would be at sea level; I can see it from the coloration of the rocks. And you could take a boat right in there, if it was calm.

So that's it. Sligo has discovered that you can get from Jacob's field down to the sea. He made a mistake in putting the new cover and lock over the shaft though; I wouldn't have pieced it together if it wasn't for that. I feel as excited as my damaged brain will allow, which is to say a mild sense of this being a good thing.

'Seen something?' the dad asks me, and it surprises me as I had forgotten they were there on the boat with me.

'Not really,' I say, turning round. 'Oh look, the Carracks. That's Seal Island.'

'Those rocks?' The dad looks disbelieving. 'That's not an island.'

'No, I suppose not,' I say. I expect everyone who reads the signs on the harbour for trips to Seal Island thinks this when they arrive here. I'm really hoping there will be some seals though, or it's going to be a let-down for them, especially the boy.

The skipper cuts the engine and we glide in amongst the rocks. They're black and slick like oil when the water splashes up over them. They always give me the creeps, especially when it's overcast like today and you can't see below the surface of the water. I'm always waiting for a rock to slice open the keel of the boat like a can opener.

'Over there,' I say, pointing.

'Oh yeah.' The dad points at the rocks where a large bull seal is lolloping just out of the water.

'And there, and there,' the boy is saying, very excited now. 'Look at that one, he's so fat!'

'Keeps them warm,' the dad says, laughing.

It takes me longer to see the others after spotting the first one, then one moves right into the centre of my field of vision and its outline emerges like the fuzzy pictures that you have to go slightly cross-eyed to see, hidden images coming out of their camouflage.

Another smaller seal flops clumsily off the rock into the water and darts alongside the boat, transformed, moving now like mercury. It pops its Labrador head out of the water near the boy and he's beside himself, waving and saying hello to it.

We stay for a little longer, the seals playing up to the visit, shooting like torpedoes alongside the boat just under the surface of the water. Then the skipper pokes his head out.

'Shall we catch some fish?'

'Yes!' the boy shouts, throwing his arms in the air. I'm pleased, he's really having fun.

'Hold on to your seats,' the skipper shouts, playing into the boy's excitement now, and opening the throttle, making the boat surge forward and us slide back.

About halfway back to St Ives the skipper cuts the engine and hands round sticks wound with fishing line and a good-sized lead weight.

'Right, lower them down and mind your hands on the hooks as you go.'

My line is hardly in the water before it starts to tremble in my hand and I know that the fish are on it.

'The line's shaking a bit,' the dad says, sounding unsure. The skipper puts his hand on the line.

'Yeah, you've got a bite. Pull it up.'

We both pull at the same time and the silver flash of mackerel sparkles in the gloom below, then another, and another. I pull them up and into the boat, the fish writhing hopelessly on the line. Grabbing them one at a time and holding them firm, I take out the hooks from their mouths as they squirm in my hand. Their skin shimmers as bright and shiny as silver, their bellies blue and emerald green, eyes bright and alert. I put them into the box in the middle of the boat and watch as the skin fades to a steely sheen and the eyes mist over, the bodies convulsing occasionally with the final thrusts of life. I rinse my hands in the sea but some of the scales remain, flecks of silver leaf.

'You going again?' the skipper asks me.

'No, that'll do. It's just me and my uncle.'

'Fair do's.'

The boy is looking into the box, his face unreadable.

'Are they dead now?' he asks, looking at my three fish and their two.

'Just about,' the dad says. 'But they didn't feel anything.'

The skipper hands me a length of twine with a thick needle on it and I thread it through the gills of two of the fish and tie it into a loop so I can carry them home.

'You cooking tonight?' the dad asks me.

'Looks that way,' I say.

'How will you do it? Not sure I'd know where to start.'

'It's really easy,' I say, passing him the twine. 'You have to gut them first. Just cut along the belly and take out the insides then throw those away. Bit of oil and salt on the skin and grill or fry it either side for a few minutes. That's it.'

'Thanks. I think we could manage that, don't you?' he says, turning to his son, who looks slightly green.

'You can,' he says.

Back on the quay, I say goodbye and head off towards Fore Street, thinking I'll drop into the bookshop in case Sophie's working.

I see her through the window as soon as I get there.

'Hello,' she says as I come into the shop. 'What are you doing in town?'

I hold up the fish.

'Lovely,' she says. 'Do you want a carrier for those if you're getting the bus?'

'Oh, yeah, good idea,' I say, laughing. 'I just came in to say I got your note, and yeah, come on Saturday.'

'I will. I'm here in the morning so I'll come after, about half one?'

'Great. Don't eat, we'll do some lunch.'

'Oh, I don't want you to bother with that.'

'Yeah, we will. I want to.'

'Fine, but I'm bringing cake. Have you got the same number?' she asks, picking up her phone.

'Oh, I haven't. I lost my phone when I was in hospital and didn't get a new one.'

'You're not turning into an off-gridder like Jacob, are you?' she says.

It's weird talking to Sophie like this. It feels like we're flirting with each other, but it's not the same as before.

'I'm not sure,' I say. 'Maybe.'

'Hmm. See you on Saturday.'

17

'Delicious,' Jacob says, wiping his mouth with a napkin and sitting back in his chair. 'That's the only way to have mackerel, fresh out of the sea. Well, some like it smoked, I suppose, but it's not to my taste.'

'Me neither,' I say, remembering the stench when my mum did poached smoked mackerel for her breakfast.

Jacob had come in from the farm just as I was filleting the fish.

'Didn't realise you were out today.'

'I hadn't planned to be,' I said. 'But I woke up late and thought I'd better do something with the day.'

I hate not telling Jacob the truth, even if it is only white lies.

'Well, I'm glad you did, that was excellent.'

'Good.'

It was nice, too. I'm getting better at cooking now. When I came out of hospital I didn't cook at all. When I tried I kept getting things wrong, getting overwhelmed, burning stuff, or confusing the quantities. Now I can do some things but they have to be simple. I don't cook instinctively any more. I need my systems, lists and timers. I can only do one thing at once and if there's too much stuff on the sideboard I can't see any of it, like not being able to see the wood for the trees. I chop an onion, put it in a bowl, put it aside, chop the next thing, put it in a bowl, and so on. It's the sort of cooking I didn't used to think was cooking at all, to be honest, but it works for me now.

The mackerel was easy, though. I put some potatoes in the stove when I got back, cut into cubes and rolled around in some oil and salt. Then I gutted the fish, fried it in loads of foamy butter, nutty brown by the end, chucked in a few capers and that was it. Fresh fish is good because the less you mess with it the better it tastes.

'I'm going to bed,' I say after washing up. The fatigue has hit me. My head hurts and I feel sick, close to shouting at Jacob for no reason at all.

'Quieter day tomorrow,' Jacob says, more as a direction than a question.

'Definitely,' I say, putting my hand on his shoulder as I walk behind his chair. It is this part of the brain injury that gets me down a bit. By any normal standards I've had a relaxing day, but the effort of talking to strangers, the noise of the boat, the brightness of the light on the sea, the journey on the bus, and the cooking have done me in. In bed I start to think about the cliff and the opening at the bottom of it, then I'm asleep.

It's early when I wake, early for me anyway. Eight o'clock. I've slept for almost twelve hours. I'm glad to hear Jacob downstairs as I want to see him. While I know he doesn't mind at all, I always feel bad when I'm too tired to talk to him as I was last night.

'I thought I heard you,' he says as I come down the stairs. 'There's bacon and toast.'

'Great, I'm starving.' This is another thing when I've overdone it. I can eat and eat and eat.

'You look a bit brighter this morning.'

'I'm fine, just did a bit too much yesterday, that's all.'

'Quiet today, is it?' he asks.

'Yeah. I thought I might go and say hello to Granny Carne later maybe.'

'All right.'

I can tell he thinks I shouldn't, that I should just stay here on my own today, and I know he's right. The more layers of fatigue I build up, the harder it is to peel them off again, but I have to talk to her. When I woke up this morning, everything seemed to have come together in my head, and I've had an idea that I need to tell her about.

Down in the field I call to Connor and he trots over eagerly. Niamh and Ruby are there too, Ruby still staying close to her mother. She's bigger though, her legs no longer having that spindly appearance. She's contained and graceful in her movement.

I lead Connor up the field, into the stable, saddle him up and we're off. It's a nice day, the sky a sharp clear blue, the air cool but not cold. The sun is milky, no longer the ball of scorching heat that it was back in the summer.

We're only a short way up the lane when a figure rounds the corner a little further up and I know immediately who it is. I don't need to see his face; I can tell from his broad shoulders and slouching walk. It's Bill Sligo.

I can't turn back, it would be too obvious. When we reach each other I'll nod. That's my plan. We're still a good twenty yards apart when he calls out. 'Your uncle home?'

'Not sure,' I say.

'I want to talk to him.' He's right in front of me now, blocking my way.

'Well, I don't know if he's home.'

'Is he going to sell me that field?'

I'm surprised that he's talking to me about it, and I have to think for a moment before deciding what to say.

'I asked you a question.'

'You'll have to ask him,' I say as steadily as I can, a thread of anger running through me.

'I intend to,' he says, looking straight at me, his grey eyes making me think of the dead mackerels from yesterday.

At this, we pass each other and I give Connor a nudge in his flank to speed him up as an unpleasant shiver passes up my spine. I can feel him watching me go. Once I'm sure he will have rounded the corner, I pause for a moment. Should I go back to make sure Jacob is OK? But of course he is. Sligo won't do anything to him now, in broad daylight.

He's not going to like it, though, when Jacob tells him he's not selling. Maybe he'll up his offer; not that that would make any difference to Jacob. People like Bill Sligo can't get their heads around people like Jacob who don't care about money.

Connor and I carry on up the lane. The hedgerows on either side have shed their summer decoration and only tight fists of brown shrivelled blackberries remain. They're still thick with evergreen leaves, though, and with brambles and gorse. A line from a Christmas poem comes into my head. *There was no berry on the bramble, only the thorn, and the cold wind whistling the night he was born.*

It'll be Christmas soon and the thought of it makes me sad. No, not sad exactly, but regretful. I loved Christmas, I always did. Christmas films, *The Snowman* on TV, then when I got older, meeting my friends in the crowded warm pub on Christmas Eve and a swim in the sea on Christmas morning. I still like the thought of it, but as with so many other things – swimming in the sea, running, a sunny morning, a snowy day, a great meal – I don't have an emotional connection to it. 'Blunted emotional response', they call it, and it's bang on as a description.

I'm glad to see a thin ribbon of smoke rising from the chimney of Granny Carne's cottage. She's home, or nearby at least. I tether Connor and make my way up the path through her garden, which is no longer a tapestry of bright colour, but a blanket of mulch feeding the soil for next year.

'It's open,' I hear her calling before my hand reaches the knocker. When I come in and close the door behind me I have to wait as my eyes adjust. Without sunlight coming through the tiny windows it's gloomy but cosy like the inside of an old-fashioned gypsy caravan, the only light coming from two oil lamps and the small flickering fire. The scrape of the kettle being taken off the stove top draws my eyes to Granny Carne. She looks smaller when she is standing, but strong as she easily lifts the cast-iron kettle to pour.

'You're frettin',' she says without turning. 'Fetch that tin down, will you?' she asks, pointing to the highest shelf above the stove.

'Open it, then,' she says while pouring steaming water into the teapot. A sweet smell of almonds with a trace of lemon wafts out of the tin. I love Madeira cake. It's my second favourite after lemon drizzle, then chocolate third.

'Yes, you're frettin'. I feel it. I see it.'

She looks up at me now for the first time since I came in, her sharp blue eyes flashing in the dim light, like a cat's eyes at night.

'Sit.'

I do as she says and she brings over the tea and two slices of the cake.

'The thing is,' I start, and then stop again. The idea of saying anything at all about her dead nephew now seems like a terrible idea. I've got to though; this is too important not to.

'The thing is . . .' I say again, then pause like a car misfiring. 'Well, I think Bill Sligo is up to something.'

'No doubt about it,' Granny Carne says.

I take a deep breath to process what she has just said.

'Do you mean something specifically, or just generally?' I ask.

'Well, both of course.'

'Right,' I say. 'Well, you know how he wants to buy Jacob's bottom field, the one by the coast path, the one with the mineshaft on it?'

'Hawk's Point. Yes, I know.' This makes me pause again. I never knew the mine had a name.

'Well, I think I know why.'

She doesn't say anything to this, but pours the tea without taking her eyes off me.

'I think he wants to use it to smuggle drugs. You see, this gang got caught, and I think he is trying to, well, fill the gap in the market if you like. I've seen him signalling to a boat and he's put a new cover over the mineshaft with a padlock.' I realise I've gone too fast and I'm not explaining things properly.

'Sorry,' I say, 'that doesn't make any sense. Let me start again.' This time, I take my notebook out and open it at the list I made of what I think is going on. I go through it all, slowly and with all the proper detail: how I found the new cover on the mineshaft; how I saw someone going down through Jacob's farm that night; how I saw someone again and followed them; and how I saw that it was Sligo signalling to a boat. I tell her about the time I went up to his farm and about the car trying to force me off the road, and the farmer's wife who helped me and told me that Bill Sligo had been a drug dealer in the past. I stop now to check my list.

'Oh, and I went out on one of the mackerel boats and there's an entrance in the cliff directly below the mine, right at sea level.' I pause and take a breath. 'That's everything,' I say, half to Granny Carne and half to myself.

'Quite the detective, aren't you?' she says, but she isn't smiling. 'And what do you intend to do with your findings?'

'Well, I'm going to catch him at it and get the police on to him. He needs to be locked up, not just for the drugs, but, well . . .' I look at her, unsure how to say it.

'Go on,' she says quietly.

'For what he did to your nephew.'

Her face darkens, truly as if black thunder clouds have gathered over her head. Her usual warm, open expression closes and her eyes flash with danger. I'm afraid, not just that I've gone too far, but as though anything could happen in the next moment.

I watch intently as she looks down into her lap, her face hidden from me now. I'm holding my breath. Then she leans forward, cuts another slice of cake and puts it on my plate. When she looks up at me her face has softened again.

'You're a kind boy, Jago,' she says. 'A kind, kind boy. But you're also a fool. Bill Sligo is as sly as a fox and as rough as a dog. You can't understand because it's not in your nature to understand a person like that.'

'I know what I've got isn't proof of anything, not proper proof,' I say quickly, 'but if I can witness him bringing drugs up the mineshaft, even take photos, and give them to the police, they'll have to arrest him. They might even catch him red-handed, and even if they don't and he denies it and there's a trial, I can be a witness. I'd like to be a witness.' I can hear my own voice rising, but still I plough on.

'He'd have to go to prison for importing drugs, and I know it's not like that would be a punishment for what he did to your nephew, for having killed him, but it would be prison, and he'd deserve it.'

'That he would, but you're not listening to me, Jago. And you must listen to me more now than at any other time I've ever spoken to you or probably ever will. Are you listening to me?'

'Yes,' I say, afraid again.

'He will kill you, Jago. Are you hearing what I'm saying

to you?' Her eyes are alive, connecting with mine as if she's trying to read my mind.

'Yes.'

'Really kill you, I mean. He wouldn't think twice about it if you got in his way. When you're not expecting it, he'll take you. You've come back from the dead once before, Jago, and you won't get that chance again.'

'Yes,' I say, almost in a whisper.

'I've asked you to make a promise to me before, Jago. Do you remember that?'

'Sort of,' I say, aware that I did promise something to do with staying away from Sligo, but I don't remember exactly what it was so I'm not sure if I've broken the promise or not.

'Well, this time I need you to swear it.'

She pushes herself up and out of her chair and goes over to the dresser, takes something out of one of the drawers, and comes back over to me with whatever it is hidden in her fist.

'Take this in your hand,' she says.

She holds out her hand. It's a locket, a gold one.

'Open it,' she says. Inside is a small lock of hair tied with a crimson ribbon.

'You're going to swear to me with Cadan Carne, my nephew, as a witness that you won't go near that man, ever. All right?'

I nod in reply.

'And if you break your oath, I'll know it,' she says.

She knows that is enough. No need for bargains – if you break the oath I won't see you again, or anything like that.

'Do you believe what I'm saying to you?'

'I do,' I say.

'Then swear it.' She closes my hand over the locket, and places her hands around mine.

'I swear I won't go anywhere near Bill Sligo.'

'Ever,' Granny Carne says.

'Ever,' I say.

'And don't even think about that man no more. He'll get his comeuppance, don't you worry.'

'But how?' I say.

'I see everything from up here, Jago, and I watch that man going up and down there thinking he's so clever mud don't stick. Well, it does, and you're not the only one with their eye on him. One of these days he'll make a mistake and I'll be watching.'

She sits back in her chair. 'Now, that's enough of that; it doesn't do to dwell on bad people or bad things, Jago. It poisons your soul in the end. Better to focus on the light.'

18

Sophie came on Saturday as she said she would, driving up in her ancient Ford Escort with its fluffy seat covers. I got up quite early to milk the cows and to make bread for lunch. I just do a simple white loaf with a cup of granary flour to give it a bit of bite. I kneaded the dough then covered it with a tea towel and left it to rise by the stove. Then I started on the soup. French onion, which I knew both Sophie and Jacob would like. It's a good one for me to do because you make it and then leave it on the stove for ages, so I had plenty of time for a rest between cooking and her arriving.

I sliced five big onions and then used a razor blade to cut very thin slivers of garlic so fine I could almost see through them. I put a big knob of butter into the heavy pan and waited until it was foaming before putting in the onions and garlic. You have to be patient with the onions, cooking them slowly until they're soft and nutty brown but not burnt. Then a big splosh of brandy, which I lit and left to burn itself out, before the white wine and finally thick beef stock. After that I had a snooze in the armchair by the fire while Jacob was still out in the fields.

I woke and put the loaf into the stove and by the time Sophie arrived and Jacob was back, the room was full of the deep sweetness of the soup and the yeasty smell of the fresh loaf, and the windows were all steamed up. I was nervous before she arrived, but that disappeared when she got here.

She really liked the lunch and was impressed with the bread, and I was glad. Jacob didn't stay with us for long. He headed back out after lunch and Sophie made some coffee for us to have by the fire as I was pretty tired by then.

Now we're on the sofa and talking and talking as if we're stitching up the hole in time from when we were apart.

'Where's the bracelet I made for you?' she asks, picking up my wrist.

'I'm really sorry,' I say. 'I caught it on something when I was on the boat in Bristol and it came off. I tried to grab it, but it was gone. I was gutted.'

'It's all right. I'll make you another.'

'Will you?'

'Of course I will.'

'So you don't hate me then?'

'Don't be stupid, and don't fish. It's annoying. Of course I don't hate you. But I do want you to know what it was like for me because it's not fair if you don't. I know we talked about it when you left, and you had to do it really. I know you did. But it was still horrible. There was nothing wrong with our relationship and you just left. And I was here and you were there and it was just . . . horrible.'

'I know,' I say. 'You know, I missed you all the time. I've thought about it so much since being ill. What's happened to me has changed me a lot. Like the way I think about things, about people. This will sound weird, but I feel like I see other people's perspectives more easily now.'

'You mean you're more compassionate?'

'I think so, yeah. I can really see what I did now and how badly I messed it all up, and I'm so sorry.'

'It's not like you weren't compassionate before. You've always been really kind and thoughtful, but you were careless with me then and I think it hurt all the more because it wasn't like you, because the Jago I know wouldn't do that.'

'All I can say is I really wasn't myself. I lost the plot after Mum died and I made all sorts of strange decisions. I mean, I don't want to live in Bristol. I was just escaping, but I sold the cottage and bought a flat and ended things with you. You know, they said to me in rehab that I shouldn't make any major decisions for at least a couple of years. That should be a rule for after people die too because I wasn't thinking straight at all back then.'

'But you said the other day you might go back to Bristol.'

'Did I? I'm not good at reacting to things in the moment any more. I need time for things to sink in. I'm not going back there. I don't know how long Jacob will let me stay here, but I'm not going back to Bristol.'

'So have you had time to think about me? About us?'

'Of course I have. Loads.'

'And?'

'I wish I could just rub out the past two years and go back to how it was before.'

'That's not an answer.'

'I know. Look, I never stopped loving you. I made a massive mistake and I can't undo it. I want us to start again. But even if you wanted that too, I'm not the same as before. I am, but I'm not. I've a got a brain injury. I'm disabled. It's so weird saying it, but that's how it is. There's loads of stuff

I can't do. So even if you did want to get back together, it wouldn't be the same.'

'But do you still love me?'

'Of course I do,' I say.

'Me too,' she says. 'And you know, what happened to you has changed me too. I've been so angry with you, and hurt, but when I heard you had nearly died I was sick. I might not have been able to get over you leaving before, but after what's happened I don't see the point in looking at the past like that.'

'That's what Jacob thinks,' I say.

'Well then,' she says, 'let's not,' and she leans towards me and we kiss, and this time it's much more than an echo of feeling. My whole body fizzes.

'Shall we go upstairs?' I say.

She nods.

She's leaning on her side, the candlelight casting shadows under the curve of her breasts, and she's running her fingers over the long scar down the middle of my chest.

'I hate that they did this to you,' she says.

'I know, but they had to, and it doesn't matter.'

She kisses me all down the scar and I run my hand over her breasts, and the feelings that I was afraid might be gone forever burst back to life.

Back downstairs, the logs in the fire have slumped down and the light outside has almost completely gone. Jacob's still not back.

'When will I see you again?' I ask Sophie as she gets into her car.

'I'm going away with Mum and Dad tomorrow. We're going to my aunt in Cumbria until after Christmas.'

'Oh, when will you be back?'

'The day after Boxing Day.'

She can see I'm disappointed.

'It won't be long,' she says. 'I'll come here on the twenty-eighth. If you want me to.'

'Definitely,' I say, and we kiss again and then the tail-lights of her car are bouncing away up the lane.

It feels really empty in the house after she's gone in a way it never has before, and I'm relieved when I hear Jacob at the door, and I know he was waiting all this time for her to leave.

19

A week has passed since then. A bitter wind bringing sleet and occasional snow has been whipping off the sea for days. Smoke races horizontally from the chimney stack and the horses huddle in the corner of the field, the cows now in the barn for the winter. During the days we've been building a dry-stone wall along one side of the kitchen garden. The idea is to shelter it better from the wind to be able to grow more delicate crops there next year.

There was a pile of rocks behind the barn that we're using for it, and the first job was to move them all around to where we're doing the wall. I start the days with my coat, my Aran jumper, T-shirt, hat and gloves, peeling off the layers as the mornings have gone on and we've moved wheelbarrow after wheelbarrow of rocks to the site of the wall.

We started doing work on it the day after Sophie came and I told Jacob about how we were getting back together. I knew he wouldn't ask as he would never force a conversation like that.

'I am pleased to hear that,' he said. 'She's a lovely girl. Your mum was very fond of her, you know.'

'I know,' I say. 'They got on really well.'

'Well, I think it's great news,' Jacob said. 'Will we be seeing her again soon?'

'Not 'til the twenty-eighth,' I say. 'She's going away with her parents for Christmas.'

'Ah well, that will come round soon enough.'

It was satisfying work doing the wall because it didn't need to be perfect. It can't be perfect really, it's just stones slotted together. But there is an art to it. The trick is to find ones that will kind of knit together nicely, and because it doesn't need to be precise measurements or anything like that I found I could do quite a good job on it.

And I liked the feeling at the end of the day, sitting by the fire, every muscle aching in a nice way. It also kept my mind off Granny Carne and Bill Sligo. A couple of days after that afternoon with Granny Carne, I remembered my encounter with Sligo on the track on the way to see her, when he had asked whether Jacob was at home. It had disappeared from my mind but had obviously lodged there somewhere, hiding out of sight. I mentioned it to Jacob, sort of in passing as we were working. I didn't say I had spoken to Sligo, just that I had seen him on the lane and had he come here?

'Yeah, he came.'

'What did he want?'

'Going on about that field again.'

'What did you say?'

'I told him to leave it alone.'

'And?'

'And that's that.' He looked up at me then and said, 'Nothing for you to be worrying about, all right?'

'All right,' I said, but I'm really uneasy about it. I feel Bill Sligo's menace stretching out like tentacles over us, but Jacob is ignoring it and I've made my vow to Granny Carne.

We finished the wall a couple of days ago, and I've been busying myself with the animals, especially Ruby who seems to be bigger every time I look at her. She's still taking Niamh's milk, but also quite a bit of grain and grass now too. She has grown out of her Bambi legs and walks confidently alongside her mother. She's strong like Niamh, but she's a long way off taking the saddle, less still pulling the cart.

She's playful, dancing around Niamh and running a little with Connor. Niamh doesn't play. She's far too grand for that sort of thing. She stands like a statue, facing down the wind, daring it to blow harder.

I muck out the stable while the horses are out. I like the smell of it and the feeling of making their space clean and comfortable. After I've swept it really carefully and washed it down with water and the stiff brush, I scatter fresh straw over the floor in small heaps that let off billows of dust as they settle, and I fill the manger with armfuls of fresh hay. We keep the manure for fertilising the beds. That's what the farm is really, a series of life cycles within life cycles, and I like being part of it. But my normal contentment is being tested by the constant presence of Sligo in my mind and in the pit of my stomach.

I think about Granny Carne's words. *He'll kill you.* I think about how unlikely that seems, but then I also think about how some people are just bad.

Earlier, when I was making a fire, I went to the bottom of the pile of newspapers to look for the article about that drug ring being caught by the police in Penzance. I found it after a while, still on the page of the article where Jacob had stopped reading. *Police describe the raid as a major disruption of a drug-importing racket thought to be worth £10 million annually.* If that is what Sligo and those other men are after, what would his share be? Two million? Maybe more. Would that be enough to make him kill someone? Well, he killed Cadan Carne over an argument in the pub. The thought of it, of Sligo doing that, makes me feel sick all over again.

20

'Morning,' I say, coming down the stairs a week later. 'What's all this?' There are three well-used cardboard boxes on the table.

'Christmas decorations,' Jacob says. 'I don't usually bother on my own but with two of us I thought we might get a bit festive.'

'Yeah, nice,' I say as enthusiastically as I can. 'What have you got then?'

'Well, I'm not sure; it's been that long since I last had these out.'

I open one of the boxes and pull out the strands of red and gold tinsel, and below them a load of coloured baubles.

'They're just like the ones we had on the tree when I was little. Have you got any lights?' I ask.

'Think so,' Jacob says. 'Try the other box. We'll be needing a tree, won't we? We'll go up to the Williamses' farm after we've had some breakfast. I've reserved a bird for Christmas Day too. A goose. Denzil up at Hope Farm is doing them. It'll be quite the feast for the two of us.'

'Sounds great.'

'Right, breakfast? I've got bacon and eggs.'

'Yes, please,' I say. 'I'll make some coffee.'

'We could go to midnight mass, you know,' Jacob says

over his shoulder. 'It's years since I've done that. They used to do it by candlelight up at the chapel. I'm not sure if that's still the case, but we could look in perhaps?'

'Great,' I say, thinking that there is no way I could stay up that late and be able to cope with Christmas Day, but I don't want to dampen the moment.

'Second thoughts,' Jacob says, 'that might be a bit late. We'd both be wiped out on Christmas Day. I'm not much of a one for church anyhow.'

'Yeah, OK,' I say, knowing that Jacob often stays up that late and then gets up at dawn no problem.

Midnight mass is one of my favourite things about Christmas. Walking to church and looking at people's trees lit up in their front rooms, no cars on the roads, everyone saying hello to each other as you come up to the church, and the waft of incense as you go in, the air slightly fogged from the smoke of it. Then the mass itself, the readings of the Christmas story, the lighting of the Christmas candle on the wreath, and the mass always ending with 'Hark! the herald angels sing' every year. The vibration from the organ would go right through me, sending shivers up my spine, and everyone would belt it out at the top of their voices. On the way home, my mum would press a little Christmas chocolate into my hand. Then into bed, too tired to even stay awake to wait for Father Christmas. We'll see. Maybe if I have a long sleep in the afternoon on Christmas Eve, I might be able to manage it.

After breakfast, I wash up and we set off in Jacob's battered, ancient Land Rover. It has hardly any suspension so you have to lift your bum off the seat slightly when going over potholes to save your spine from shooting through your brain. Her, I should say. Jacob calls her Bertha and speaks to her like she's an old lady. 'Come on, old girl,' he says every time we set off in her, 'let's hit the road once more.' She's one of Jacob's very few concessions to the modern world.

It's also freezing cold as Bertha's heating has not worked for years, so I sit on my hands both to warm them and to help cushion the blows from the chassis as we drive up the lane.

The Williamses' farm is at the top of the hill that runs along the ridge of the peninsula, and as we rise up we get good views across the fields and stretches of uneven, unfarmed land. It's carpeted with heather and dotted with scraggy gorse bushes hunched close to the land and slanting away from the direction of the wind, their bare branches spindly like witches' fingers.

'Looks like snow,' Jacob shouts over the diesel chug of the engine. I lean forward to look up out of the windscreen. The sky is thick with heavy grey clouds, each indistinguishable from the other. Up ahead, wisps of cloud break away and stroke the land.

A few flecks of snow land on the windscreen; then the sky opens and waves of snowflakes wash over the hill, beginning to settle straight away on the frozen ground. When we get to the farm, half an inch has settled already. And when I open my door I'm hit by the raw wind and the sweet smell of new snow.

'This way,' Jacob says, pointing at a sign shaped like a Christmas tree.

This farm is much bigger than Jacob's, with proper corrugated iron barns, not at all like Jacob's granite buildings. We walk quickly over the car-park-type area, the wind pushing us back, and round the corner of the barn, where it's more sheltered.

There are a lot of trees, some on display in stands, others heaped up in their nets. It would all look a bit bleak if it wasn't for the snow, which makes it seem more Christmassy.

We go over to a man in overalls and a woolly hat who's dragging trees from one side of the yard to the other.

'All right, Jacob,' he says as he looks over to see who's coming.

'All right, John.'

'Gettin' yourself a tree this year, are you? Not like you, you tight bugger,' he says, laughing.

'Well, I've got young Jago with me this year, so I thought we'd make a bit of an effort.'

'Your boy?' John asks, sounding surprised.

'No, Jago's my nephew. Jago Trevarno, John Williams,' Jacob says.

'All right, Jago. What you after then, Jacob?'

'Nothing too mad,' Jacob says, 'six foot or so?'

'Oh yeah, I got some real beauties.'

'Course you 'ave,' Jacob says.

'Follow me, gentlemen.'

We walk together over to the corner of the yard where the netted trees are piled up and John starts sorting through them, pulling three out after a while and then slinging them near our feet. He cuts the netting as if filleting fish and holds them up one by one for us to inspect, giving them a good bang on the ground to even out the branches.

The first one is too patchy, the second one too thin, but

the third is perfect. Quite fat, good triangle shape and bushy, none of the trunk visible at all, except for the little bit at the top.

'What do you think?' Jacob asks me.

'Number three for sure,' I say.

'Good lad,' John says, 'she's a beaut all right.'

'Can I pay for it?' I ask Jacob while John is feeding the tree back through the hoop thing that puts the netting on like a sausage machine.

'If you like,' Jacob says. 'You sure?'

'Yeah, I'd like to,' I say.

I hand over the money, forty pounds, and we carry the tree to Bertha, one end each. It fits well in the back, just the end poking over the tailgate.

'I think we'd better get the goose and a few other bits now,' Jacob says, looking up at the sky. 'We might be snowed in if this carries on.'

'Do you think it will?'

'Certainly feels like it's going to be a heavy dump. Supposed to be a lot of snow and then very cold for quite a while.'

I like the sound of this, stuck inside with the fire burning, lots of food and playing chess with Jacob.

Next we pick up the goose and also get a chicken, some Cornish Yarg, a blue cheese that looks like Stilton but isn't apparently, extra-mature Cheddar, and a good slab of quince paste wrapped in waxed paper. We've got enough veg of our own. Next, we stop at Rowan Tree Farm for sausages, bacon and eggs, then the final stop is Mrs Beaton's for a bottle of brandy, a homemade Christmas cake and some mince pies. Jacob also buys a packet of rolling tobacco, just a very small one.

'I have a pipe at Christmas,' he says, seeing my surprise at him buying this.

'Oh, right,' I say, a bit amused by the idea of it.

'Although I won't if it bothers you,' he says.

'Doesn't bother me at all,' I say. I actually really like the smell of pipe smoke. It makes me think of my grandpa. Once I took half a pack of tobacco from his store and kept it in my bedroom, taking it out every now and then just to smell it. I can taste the smell of it now.

'That's us ready for anything, I should think,' Jacob says as we climb back into Bertha.

It feels nice: the snow falling, the car full of supplies, the warm farmhouse to go back to. The snow continues to chuck down on the drive back, the moorland around us barely visible through dense sheets of white. The farm looks like a Christmas card when we get back to it, two or three inches of snow already blanketing everything, the roof a sheet of white and smoke buffeting around the chimney stack.

We shake the tree off and take it inside where Jacob has ready a bucket with some rocks in it to wedge around the trunk of the tree. After a bit of jiggling to get it straight, we stand back to look at it. It really is a proper Christmas tree.

'I'll put on some coffee if you start with the lights,' Jacob says, throwing a couple of logs on to the embers in the grate, sending a shower of orange sparks out on to the hearth.

I take the lights out of one of the boxes, multi-coloured icicles, and begin to unravel them. They are tangled as Christmas lights always are. Mum would get me to do this because I could untangle even the worst birds' nests of wires. Now, though, I'm staring at the web, unsure what to do, my brain frozen. Tentatively, I pull apart a couple of strands and watch as others tighten. I can almost feel the synapses in my brain firing and missing their target, and my head fills with the familiar concrete wall that I can't get over or around. Jacob has obviously seen this as he comes over and says, 'Here, I'll do that if you want to start on the decorations?'

I start with the tinsel, which is a bit threadbare, but fine. There's a mix of red, gold, silver, purple, green and blue. There are some glittery stars, some baubles, and some little wooden reindeer as well.

'Here we are,' Jacob says, holding out the lights and a mug of coffee. As he does this I remember that the lights are supposed to go on first so the wires are more hidden, but never mind.

'There's a star in there somewhere, I think.'

'I can't see it,' I say. 'But there is this.'

I hold up an angel made of a toilet roll wrapped in foil and wings cut from a paper doily, with yellow wool for hair.

'You made that,' Jacob says.

'Do you want me to put it on?' I ask, unsure as to whether we should, as it's not good.

'Of course.'

Jacob wraps the icicle lights around and around the tree and attaches the wires to the battery pack. The lights don't shine very brightly, but it's dusk outside and they look good in the fading light.

'Nice!' I say.

'Yeah, not bad.'

For dinner we have beef and ale casserole with dumplings that Jacob makes from scratch and jacket potatoes rubbed with oil and sprinkled with crystals of sea salt to make the skin extra crispy.

I go up to bed early after dinner, tired from the day. I sit in my window seat for a while, a candle burning on my bedside table, watching the snow still swirling outside. I can just about make out the blanketed ground below in the strange purplish glow of the fresh snow. I push open my window and stick out my head, cold air coming in and sinking down around my bare feet. I blow a bloom of breath out into the cold and it hangs there before dissolving into the night.

It didn't often snow in St Ives when I was little, but when it did I used to sit like this for hours, waiting for the snow to come, then watching mesmerised as it rushed through the orange glow of the street lamp outside and slowly filled the courtyard out the front of the cottage which would disappear under it. Then I'd lie in my bed, willing more snow to fall, sitting up every now and then and putting my head under the curtains to look out to check, not sleeping until the snow had stopped or I couldn't keep my eyes open any longer.

21

I wake up in the middle of the night. It's not as dark as normal in my room, but it's not the light of the moon either. I lie for a moment trying to work it out, before remembering the snow. Then I hear a noise, a shrill scream piercing the air. This must have been the noise that woke me up. I rush across my room and open the door. The hall is as black as ink and shapes appear in my vision as my brain tries to process the darkness. I feel my way to the top of the stairs and start carefully down. I stop. There's a smell. Burning. I try to think what it could be and then it comes to me. The Christmas lights. They must have caught fire somehow. I carry on down as quickly as I can, almost falling down the stairs.

Once in the kitchen I look across the room expecting to see the tree smouldering, but it's dark in that corner. Across the room from me, though, the four small squares of the kitchen windows are glowing with an orange light. I rush over to the window and look out, already the weight of dread in my stomach like stone. The side of the barn is ablaze, light from the fire dancing on the thick snow, which is still falling but lighter now. All three horses are craning their necks out of the stable door, shrieking horribly.

'Jacob!' I shout and I run to the bottom of the stairs. 'Jacob! The barn's on fire!'

I go quickly to the door, unlock it and run around the corner of the farmhouse. Flames are rolling up the side of the barn, towards the roof, and smoke is billowing out from under the rafters.

Again the horses scream, straining their heads away from the flames just metres from the stable door. I look around frantically, but I can barely see anything in this light. Shadows swallow everything but the flames and the horses' heads, which shimmer in the glow of the blaze. I don't know what to do. I'm paralysed by indecision, and I look around, desperately trying to make more sense of the scene. Then I hear Jacob's heavy footsteps as he runs to me.

'Take the horses to the field, Niamh and Ruby together, then come back for Connor.' His voice sounds calm, much calmer than I feel.

'What about the cows?' I say.

'They're in the next barn, they'll be fine. Now go!'

I don't hesitate now that I've been told what to do. I go straight to the stable door and start talking to the horses as I slide the bolts open.

'Easy now. Come on, it's all right. Come on.'

'Mind they don't bolt,' Jacob calls over to me.

I open the door just enough to slide into the stable. It's smoky inside and I pull my jumper up over my mouth as the smoke catches the back of my throat, reminding me for a moment of standing round the fire at Bonfire Night years ago. My eyes are already watering. It's almost pitch black in here. I go as quickly as I can to the back of the stable, arms stretched out in front of me, groping the dark for the tack wall. I feel leather straps and the ice-cold metal of the buckles. I'm coughing now, and I crouch down below the cloud of smoke. The air is clear here. I stand to grab the head collars from the wall, then back down again. I need to get the collars on so the horses don't bolt but there's no time to do it properly. I slip one on each horse's neck and loop them around, talking to the horses as calmly as I can all the time and smoothing their faces. Smoke is now pouring into their stalls. I'm about to open the door when I feel Connor rear up, almost lifting me off the ground, a shrill cry of panic coming from him. I can't see him, can't see where I should go to get myself out of his way. I flatten myself against the wall just as the leads slacken in my hands and I hear his hooves pound the stable floor as he comes back down. As quickly as I can I open the door, fully this time, and I go out, leading Niamh and Ruby away from the stable and the flaming barn next door.

'All right?' Jacob shouts.

'Yeah, OK,' I say between coughs and deep breaths of fresh icy air. I keep walking, afraid that if I stop before we're well away from the fire, the horses will panic. I take them over to the other side of the yard and tether them, so I can go back for Connor.

Back inside the stable, Connor is pacing around and whinnying, but when he hears my voice I sense him calm a little. I feel for his head in the dark, and find it. I hold him close to me.

'It's OK,' I say. 'It'll be over in a minute. I'll just get you out of here.'

I keep talking to him like this as I take him out. He's pulling hard on the rope, but I know it will be OK now, that he will calm down once I get him away from the fire.

After the almost pitch-blackness of the stable I can see more clearly out here. I take Connor over to the other side of the yard to join Niamh and Ruby; then I look back at Jacob. He's filling buckets from the trough and throwing them over the pile of burning firewood that's stacked up against the barn. The edge of the roof is smouldering but it looks as though the snow is stopping the fire from really taking hold of the barn itself. Still, I hurry towards the lane so I can get the horses in the end field and then help Jacob.

Once out of the gate, I look to the right, up the lane, wondering for a moment whether I should go and get help. But no, by the time I could get to the village and find someone the fire will have taken the roof at least. I turn left into the lane that goes down to the field, and as I do this I think I see something move in the shadows. I stop and stare hard into the darkness. Nothing. Quickly, I lead the horses down to the gate. It's hard work going through the snow, like wading through water. I heave the gate against the snow, which is banked up against it, making a quarter-circle like a snow plough.

'Wait here,' I say to the horses, and I hurry back to Jacob.

'Pump more water,' he calls. I do long sweeping pumps and watch as the water gushes into the trough. As I'm doing this I look over to Jacob and the fire. It's almost beautiful, the light of the fire making the snow seem to move like a rough sea.

'All right, that's enough, get the pail and chuck the water under the rafters.'

I look up to see the flames have moved along the timbers on the underside of the roof. I throw bucket after bucket up there, starting at the part that's least on fire and moving towards where the flames are bedding in. Jacob is tackling the burning pile of firewood at the same time. I think I'm going quite quickly, but he's really going, dashing between the trough and the barn. Bit by bit we start to win, blazing wood turning black, wet and steaming. When the fire is almost completely out, it's much darker out here and Jacob asks me to go inside to get some lanterns.

When I come back all the light from the fire has gone entirely and the lanterns alone now cast pools of yellow light on the snow around us. I pass a lantern to Jacob and he holds it up to the roof. The roof itself is still mostly covered with snow, and looks intact, but the underside of it is heavily charred. Inside, the barn is smoky but we can see enough to know that there's no major damage. Outside, half of the firewood that was stacked up has crumpled down into ashes, but the stuff further back is all right.

'Could have been a lot worse,' Jacob says, wiping sweat off his forehead with his sleeve.

He goes to the stable and puts his head in. 'Smoky,' he says.

'Shall we leave them in the fields for the rest of the night?' I asked. 'I can take their rugs down to them.'

'No,' Jacob says. 'Whoever's done this might still be around. I'm not risking it. We'll put them in the yard with the gate closed.'

'What?' I say, shocked. 'You think someone did this on purpose?'

'Oh yes. Can't you smell that?'

I sniff. It smells of bonfires the day after, but there is another smell too. And I can't think what it is.

'Petrol,' Jacob says.

'But who would do that?' I ask, my brain catching up with my mouth as I say it.

'You can't think of anyone?'

'Yes,' I say. 'I can.'

'Come with me,' Jacob says.

We walk around the side of the barn to the back. Sure enough, there are tracks where someone has waded through the snow.

'Shall we follow the footsteps?' I ask.

'No point,' Jacob says. 'He'll have gone to the lane a bit further up, and from there to the road.'

'Yeah, but no one will have been out, or hardly anyone. We could follow the tracks all the way to his farm and then we'll know for sure.'

'I think we know enough,' Jacob says. 'Let's get the horses back into the yard and check on the cows.'

We make our way down the lane and into the field. Either the snow or fear has kept the horses from going anywhere. They're in a huddle just by the fence.

'Your teeth are chattering,' Jacob says as we make our way back up the lane with Niamh, Ruby and Connor.

'Yeah,' I say, feeling it for the first time. My legs are wet from the sloshing water, and my back is damp with cold sweat. We get the horses back into the yard, put their rugs on, then close the gate and go into the kitchen. The fire in the wood burner is almost dead, but coming into the farmhouse still feels like getting into a warm bath.

Jacob pokes and blows at the embers, throws on a handful of kindling and some logs, then goes over to fill the kettle.

'No, you stay there,' he says when I get up to help him. 'Here, you can toast these.' He holds out four crumpets in one hand and the toasting fork in the other. Already the fire has burst back to life. I hold my hands close to the flames for a minute and then start toasting the crumpets. I'm ravenous.

'I don't understand why, though,' I say, looking over to Jacob, who is filling the teapot with boiling water. 'Why would he do that? What's the point?'

'Well,' Jacob says, putting down a tray with the teacups, plates, knives, butter and bramble jam. 'First, I think we can definitely say it wasn't kids messing around. It's the middle of the night; we're set back from the road; there's only one set of tracks. Why would Sligo do it? Well, one of two reasons. No, three. First, he's angry that I haven't sold the field to him and he wants some sort of revenge. He is that kind of person. Vindictive. I doubt it's revenge he's after really, though, because it was a bit half-hearted.'

'What?' I say, shocked at this. 'He set fire to the barn.'

'Well, he didn't really. He set fire to a stack of wood by the barn. The barn itself is damaged, true, but not too badly. If he wanted it to have been worse, it would have been.'

'Yeah, but if we hadn't woken up, the fire would have taken the stable too. He obviously didn't care what happened to the horses.'

'I don't imagine he did. But he could have chucked a can of petrol into the barn or into the stable even, and they would have gone up in minutes.'

The fire in the stove crackles as that awful thought sinks in.

'Watch it,' Jacob says, 'that crumpet's catching.' I pull it away just in time.

'OK,' I say, 'so say he thought we'd wake up before any major damage was done, what was the point then?'

'Well, second reason might be that he knows I don't put much store by money, and he might have thought I'd have to sell the field to pay for repairs.'

'Surely he'd know that if he burnt the whole place down you would rebuild it yourself. You wouldn't pay for builders to come in.'

'That's true. I've not had a tradesman on this farm in thirty years, except friends visiting, like. Anyway, as I say, there's not too much damage.'

'So, the third reason?' I ask.

'It's as a warning. A taste of what he'll do if I dig my heels in and don't budge on the field.'

The thought of this sounds worse to me than the other two options. It's a threat hanging over us like a guillotine's blade.

'What do you think he'll do now?' I ask.

'Well, I think that's the point,' Jacob says. 'He wants us to wonder what he might do, to fret on it, but we're not going to do that. Bullies need fuel to keep them going, just as much as a fire does, and we're not going to give it to him.'

We sit quietly, eating the crumpets and drinking the tea. I'm thinking through what Jacob has said but it doesn't make any sense to me. We're not talking about ignoring some name-calling in the playground and turning the other cheek. Bill Sligo could have killed the horses.

'I thought I was the one who is supposed to be pathologically apathetic,' I say at last to Jacob.

He smiles and sits back in the armchair. 'Of course I'm

bothered,' he says. 'The man's a nasty bastard, always has been, but we're not going to have any conflict with him. Either of us, do you understand me? He's not like you or me. Violence doesn't mean anything to him. We couldn't beat him in a conflict because he'd be willing to do things that you and I wouldn't contemplate. Do you get my meaning?'

'I suppose so,' I say.

'Anyway, right now you need to get to bed.'

'What about you?'

'I'll go up in a bit. I'm still a bit hungry.'

He isn't hungry; I know he isn't. He's going to stay up in case Sligo comes back. I am tired though, through and through, so I head up.

I lie in bed, exhausted but unable to sleep. The muffled sound of Jacob filling the coffee pot and putting it on the hot plate drifts up the stairs. My body is wound tight, too tight for my mind to let sleep take it. I wonder if this is how it's going to be. Jacob sitting up to watch in case Sligo comes back while making out that if we ignore him he'll get bored like a naughty boy taunting a cat. I've learned enough about Bill Sligo to know that he won't. Jacob surely knows this too, but he doesn't want the conflict. Well, come to that, nor do I, but I have the feeling of a cloud of black smoke settling over us, slowly choking us.

We have to do something.

22

When I wake it's very light in my room. Then I remember the snow, and I can smell it too, sweet cold air seeping through the cracks around the windows. It's warm under the blankets, though, and I feel cocooned and safe, the same feeling I had after waking from the coma. Then the memories of last night flood in and my body clenches.

The house is silent. Jacob must have gone to bed at last and is still asleep after staying up late. This can't carry on. How is Jacob supposed to farm if he's on guard all night?

Everything is clear to me this morning, my thoughts as sharp and as crisp as the air. Bill Sligo has to be stopped. And if we can't tackle him ourselves, we need to get the police on to him. You get years for drug-smuggling; it said so in the newspaper. They'll need evidence, though. At the moment, it's all what they call circumstantial. I need hard proof and I can only see one way of getting it.

I'm going to have to follow him when he next goes to the mineshaft, and get photos of him with the drugs when he takes delivery of them. I need a camera that takes photos in the dark, though. I'll go into St Ives today. Swinging my legs out of bed, I feel more energetic and motivated than I have since before the cardiac arrest. I wash quickly, dress and go downstairs to make some breakfast. The Christmas tree looks sad in the corner without its lights, so I go over and turn them on and something about the tree lit up loosens the tension in my stomach a little.

As I put the pan on the stove for breakfast, Jacob comes down the stairs. He looks like he slept in his clothes.

'Did you get any sleep after that?' he asks me.

'Yeah, quite a bit actually, after a while. How long did you stay up?'

'It was a while, I must say.' He sounds weary.

'You can't do that every night,' I say. The other problem with Jacob staying up to keep watch is that if I need to sneak out at night to follow Sligo, and Jacob is still up, he'll stop me for sure.

'Maybe I could do it some nights,' I say, thinking privately how staying up for just one night would write me off for a week.

'No. Kind of you, but no. Don't worry, I've had an idea actually.'

'What is it?' I ask.

'You'll see,' he says, a grin coming over his face. 'What are you doing today anyway?' he asks, changing the subject.

'Well, I'll get the horses back into the stable first, and then I thought I'd go into St Ives and pick up a couple of things for Christmas.' This is not untrue; it's just that I'll also go to the camera shop.

'Road'll be closed, I'd have thought, with all this snow.'

'Oh yeah, you're right. We need to sort out the mess from the fire anyway, so I'll stay and help you with that.'

'All right. Not much to it, though. Fortunately there's still plenty of wood left to keep us going. Loads in fact.'

'What about the roof of the barn?' I ask.

'I had another look last night. It's not too bad, just the underside at the front. That will be a job for this spring. It won't be leaking, I'm sure.'

As I'm washing up the breakfast things my mind turns straight back to my plan. With the road blocked and no thaw forecast for at least a week, I don't know how I'm going to get a camera for night photos. There's nothing for it. I'm going to have to ask Jacob.

'Do you know anything about taking photos in the dark?' I ask him over my shoulder.

'Well, it's just about the aperture and shutter speed really. Why d'you ask?'

'I was thinking about taking some photos of the snow at night,' I say, a twinge of guilt passing through me at the lie. 'But my camera is just a pocket one, though – a point-and-shoot – it's no good for night photography.'

Jacob looks at me, clearly thinking that this is an odd thing to want to do; then he gets up and goes over to the dresser.

'Well, you could try my old SLR, if you like? Look, I've even got a roll of film, too. Not sure how old it is,' he says, reading the packet, but seeming to warm up to the idea now. I know that what he's pleased about is me taking an interest in something. This also makes me feel bad.

'Do you know how to use one of these cameras?'

'Not really,' I say. 'Actually, not at all.'

He laughs. 'It's much easier than it looks. Here, this one's the aperture,' he says, pointing to a button-sized knob on the top of the camera. 'And here's the shutter speed. At night you want a nice big aperture and a slow shutter speed to let lots of light into the lens and on to the film. You have to hold the camera very still, though, else it'll be blurry, sort of like smearing paint when it's not yet dry. Get my meaning?'

'I think so,' I say.

'A tripod is best for night photography but I'm afraid I don't have one. But you can just rest it on a wall or whatever.'

'Don't I need a flash?' I ask, seeing there isn't one.

'Not for night photos, no. It's all about getting the settings right.'

'So what aperture would you use for photos outside in the snow then?'

'Try this.' He turns the dials and passes the camera back to me. 'Only trouble is, you have to wait until you develop the film before you know whether you've got it right, but I'm sure you'll get something with it set up like this.'

After this, we go to clear up the mess from the fire last night. Jacob was right, the damage is not as bad as I thought it would be. There's a lot of burnt wood on the wood pile, but really it could have been a lot worse. We chuck the burnt logs into the wheelbarrow and we take them round to the fire pit just outside the yard. We do five loads altogether; then we shovel up the ash that's left into the barrow and I put that into a metal dustbin I haven't really noticed before.

'We'll burn this lot down,' Jacob says, pointing out the charred logs, 'and use the ash for the veg patches.'

'What do you mean?' I ask.

'Soil here's acidic, so we need to balance it out every now and then, and ash is alkaline. You see, every cloud has a silver lining,' Jacob says, chuckling.

'That's true,' I say, thinking about how although my brain injury has a lot of downsides, it has its positives too.

'I've got to have a sleep,' I say, once we've finished. Doing the clearing up has distracted me from how tired I am after last night, and now fatigue hits me like a train and I must get into bed.

When I wake I can't even remember getting into bed. My mouth is dry and I have a sharp headache, right across the top of my head. It's dark in my room but with the same silvery glow from the snow as last night.

'I was going to check on you in a minute,' Jacob says as I come downstairs into the kitchen.

'How long was I asleep for?'

He looks at his watch. 'Five hours, give or take. You needed it. Hungry?'

'Very.'

'Jackets with cheese, hope that's all right,' he says, pulling four crisp dark potatoes out of the stove.

My mouth waters as I cut into the potatoes and a waft of steam hits my face. The potato skins are almost sweet where they're cooked just to the point of catching. I eat as if I haven't eaten for days. The fatigue always makes me crave food, especially carbs, fat and sugar.

'Is there pudding?' I ask.

'Apple pie,' Jacob says, smiling.

I have two slices with warm custard from a tin, and then at last I am full and very tired again. We sit for a bit by the fire. Jacob reads his book, but I just look at the Christmas tree, making my eyes go in and out of focus and blurring the lights until they're big round orbs of colour.

23

The sound of Jacob coming into the yard wakes me up the next morning. A minute later, the door downstairs opens and I hear Jacob stamping the snow off his boots. I get out of bed and put on my dressing gown, going over to the window. There was even more snow in the night. Everything is covered and smoothed over like a Christmas cake.

'Are you awake?' Jacob calls from downstairs.

'Yes,' I call back, heading over to the door.

'I've got something to show you,' he says. My stomach tightens at the thought that something bad has happened, but then I realise his tone is cheerful and I relax. In the kitchen, Jacob is crouched down with his back to me.

'Ready?' he asks.

'Yes,' I say, with no idea what he has in front of him. He moves to the side and there, on the kitchen floor, is a dog. A puppy, not a tiny one, but still young.

'What?' I say, too surprised to say anything else.

'This is Ridge, our new dog.'

'Properly ours? Like he's staying?'

'Yep. He can keep watch for us and let us know if there's anyone snooping around at night. And he'll be good company for you, too, I thought.'

'Yeah!' I say, the closest to really excited I've been all year.

'Come and say hello then.'

Ridge takes a step back when I approach him, but then comes up to me as I kneel down, and sniffs my knees.

'Nice, isn't he?' Jacob asks.

'Really nice. I love his colour.' He's jet black with a white diamond under his chin, which carries on down his neck. He's very soft when I touch him, his fur fine, and he's more solid than I was expecting.

'What is he?'

'Bit of a mix, some spaniel, a bit of retriever, something else probably. He's from John Williams – you know? Where we got the tree? They had a litter about six months ago and they held on to three of them. They were planning to keep them all but I drove up this morning and I asked if they knew of any dogs going and John said we could have this one. Said I'd be doing him a favour as having three puppies under their feet was turning out to be a bit of a pain in the end. He told me about it when we were there the other day, but we weren't in the market for a dog then. So here we are.'

'So the roads are open, are they?' I ask, thinking again about going into St Ives.

'No, but Bertha won't be stopped by anything.'

'He's great,' I say, 'look at him.' I pick Ridge up and put him on my knee; then he wriggles off and rolls over.

'He's not much of a guard dog I shouldn't have thought, but as long as he barks like mad if anyone comes snooping around that'll do me.'

'Yeah, it's a good idea,' I say, feeling a big sense of relief, like we've got a little intruder alarm.

'I thought he could sleep down here or up with you if you

like, so long as you leave your door a little bit ajar so he can hear what's going on down here, like.'

'Yeah,' I say, 'I'll do that.'

I spend most of the rest of the day playing with Ridge when he's not sleeping. He sleeps a lot. One minute he's running around in circles like mad, then he's curled up in a ball on the cushion and blanket Jacob put down for him by the hearth. He's already quite well trained from being up at the Williamses' farm. He comes when he's called, stands by the door and squeaks when he wants to go out to the loo, can sit and lie down on command. I already like him a lot.

When it comes to bedtime he follows me up the stairs, sort of lolloping up each one like a seal. I start with him on the floor but he squeaks, obviously wanting to be up here with me, so I lift him up and he curls into a ball halfway down the bed. I hadn't noticed it downstairs but he's quite a noisy sleeper. He snuffles and wriggles around a lot, standing up and doing circles on the spot before sitting down again. I don't mind that at all, though. I've wanted a dog for as long as I can remember, and I've always imagined the weight of one lying on my bed.

And actually, despite the noises and the shifting around, I fall asleep quickly. It's not long before I'm awake again, though. Ridge has managed to get off the bed and is standing by the door squeaking. I'm going to have to take him down for a wee.

Outside, it's freezing. I wrap my dressing gown around me and pull the door quickly behind me to stop the cold air pouring into the house. The sky is completely clear and the moon is almost full making the snow twinkle like a glitter ball. I go down the path a bit, which Jacob has cleared. I test the snow with my slippered foot. It's no longer soft and powdery; it has a sugary crust, which crunches under my foot.

'Come on then,' I say to Ridge, putting him down on to the path, 'time to go.' Apparently this is what they used to say to him at the farm when they were training the puppies. He hops about like he doesn't want his paws on the cold ground. After a bit of sniffing around he lifts a leg and does his wee.

I don't go straight back inside. I stand there looking at the moonlight, then up at the sky. There are millions of stars. Some brilliant pinpoints, others distant smudges of light. My mind goes back to that moment in rehab, lying on the wall in the garden, looking up at the sky, thinking everything would be all right. I knew then that it would be, and it is. I don't like the constant headaches and the tiredness, feeling sick and all that, but I can live with the rest of it all right.

I'm happy, I think. Content, at least. I like the slow, quiet days; I like being with Jacob; I like the farm; I like the animals, especially Connor, and now Ruby and Ridge who is squeaking to be picked up. I tuck him into a fold in my dressing gown; then I blow a deep breath up into the sky and watch it bloom and dissolve again.

A thought of Bill Sligo pushes in, but I push back. Everything is all right, and everything will be all right one way or another. I've already come back from the dead this year, and that wasn't too bad at all. I didn't even notice it happening. Sligo can do what he likes. We will work it out.

I put Ridge down one more time to see if he wants to go

again, but he squeaks in protest so I pick him up and go back inside. I'm expecting him to wake me up again during the night, but when I do wake up it's to the sound of Jacob in the kitchen.

'Good boy,' I say to Ridge as he does a full body stretch on the bed and yawns with his little mouth as wide as it can go.

'Christmas Eve!' Jacob says as I come into the kitchen with Ridge tucked into my dressing gown.

'Oh yeah,' I say, having forgotten or at least not having thought about that yet.

'How was the night?'

'He needed to go out once but that was it. Not sure what time that was.'

'Half eleven,' Jacob says.

'Oh, was that all? I thought it was later, like three or something. Sorry, did I wake you?'

'Oh, no bother,' he says, meaning I probably did but he wouldn't say so.

'You must be tired.'

'No more than normal,' I say, 'I usually wake up a bit in the night anyway and I always get back to sleep nice and quick so it's fine. Once is good anyway, isn't it, for a puppy?'

'Yes, I should think so. It would probably have been a lot more than that a couple of months ago.'

I play with the dog while Jacob carries on with the breakfast; then he asks, 'Did you take any photos in the end, of the snow, like?'

'Oh no, I forgot,' I say, and it's true, I did forget. I meant to try taking a few so at least I'd be following through with my story about why I wanted to use the camera. 'I'll try to take a couple tonight if I remember.'

'Good idea,' he says. 'What's your plan today? Anything?'

'No, not really, just hang around, I think.'

'You can help me get a few bits ready for tomorrow's lunch if you like.'

'Oh yeah, that would be good,' I say, pleased to be able to help a bit as usually Jacob does most things.

'You know how to make stuffing?'

'Nope.'

'Cranberry sauce?'

'Nope.'

'Well, we'll do it together,' he says, laughing. 'It's nice having you here for Christmas. Well, it's nice having you here all the time; I just mean I'm normally on my own at Christmas.'

'I'm glad too,' I say.

After breakfast I take Ridge out into the yard. He snaps at the snow, taking in mouthfuls and looking surprised each time at how cold it is. The horses are much less interested in the snow and don't particularly want to come out but Connor, Niamh and Ruby should have a bit of time in the field. Although it must be around zero degrees or a bit less, the sun has an echo of warmth. I lead them down, me taking exaggerated strides and the horses' long legs slicing through the snow.

Once in the field, straight away they canter around, kicking up the snow into shimmering silver clouds behind them. I lean on the fence, watching them play, feeling the milky winter sun on my face. Ridge had tried to follow me down, but the snow covered his legs completely and after a good few tries of leaping forwards he gave up and sat in the sun by the door.

After a while I leave the horses to it and go back to the farmhouse where Jacob is busy chopping onions with a piece of bread in his mouth.

'Does that actually work?' I ask, looking at the tears in his eyes and on his cheeks.

'I'd have to say no,' he says, taking a bite of the bread and putting the rest down on the side. 'I've always been a terrible crier when it comes to onions.'

'Shall I finish them?'

'No, you're all right. I'm almost done. You do the cranberries: chop them up as small as you can.'

I've never actually touched a cranberry before, and I'm surprised to feel how hard they are. They're like little red bullets that tinkle as I pour them from the paper bag into the glass bowl. They're fiddly to cut and it takes me ages. It reminds me of being in rehab when they asked me to make a stir fry and I was so slow slicing carrot sticks that they asked me whether I was normally like that.

'No!' I said, laughing at how delicately they were asking it.

'Well done,' Jacob says when I finally finish chopping. 'Get them into a pan and squeeze this in.' He passes me an orange.

'And a splash of this,' he says, going over to the cabinet and taking out a bottle of port. The cork squeaks and then pops as he opens it. It smells like Christmas, probably because the only time I've ever had port has been at that time of year.

'Bit of sugar, a few cloves and then we just boil it for a few minutes, *et voilà*! Cranberry sauce, and much better than that sugary nonsense in a jar.'

'Nice,' I say, holding my head over the pan and breathing it in.

'Let's just stuff the bird, then it's all ready, pretty much. We'll sort the carrots and spuds tomorrow.'

Jacob gets the goose from the cold slab in the pantry and lays it on the side.

'Well, she's certainly well refrigerated,' he says, inviting me to touch the skin, which is as cold as the marble.

'The skin's really thick,' I say, 'not at all like chicken.'

'Oh, this is much better than chicken,' he says. 'That's the fat, all that thickness, and it runs into the meat when it's cooked. My mouth's watering already.'

When we're finished, he asks if I want to play chess. 'Yeah, go on,' I say.

We play until I start making blunder after blunder, and Jacob says, 'Let's give this a rest.'

'OK,' I say. My head has begun to hurt a lot.

'You're doing really well considering you can only see a bit of the board at a time and can't remember any of it,' Jacob says.

'Thanks.'

'Cup of tea or are you having a lie-down?'

'I think I'll have a lie-down. I need to pace myself so I'm all right for tomorrow.'

'You do that, but you know, tomorrow we'll just have a quiet day with some nice food.'

I feel like crying. It rises up in me partly because of how kind Jacob is, but mainly because I'm much more tired than I thought I was. Cooking and chess have knocked me out already.

Upstairs I lie down, not really intending to sleep but I do. When I wake up, the sky is already darkening towards dusk. It looks heavy, like it might snow again.

Downstairs, the oil lamps are lit and the fire is crackling softly in the corner. The table is covered with large boughs of holly.

'Look,' Jacob says, 'I cut this off the bush to do a few sprigs around the place. I must say it didn't look like this much outside. Do you want to help? There's tea in the pot.'

I sit down and take a pair of ancient but well-oiled secateurs.

'Good holly,' I say.

'I know. It's not every year it comes out like this.'

It is dense with deep evergreen leaves and thick clusters of pillar-box-red berries.

'If we tie some string around these stalks once we've done a few bunches we can pin them to the rafters and the mantle, I thought.'

'Yeah, nice.'

'Found these too.' He passes over two packs of unmade multi-coloured paper chains.

'Not sure if this sticky will still be any good but we'll see. They must be antique. Also a bit naff, I suppose.'

'No!' I say. 'Paper chains are great. Very festive.'

Before I even pick them up I can taste the gum strip you have to lick to stick them, the memory of it pulling me back in time for a brief moment.

The room looks good once we have the sprigs on the beams and the paper chains looping down.

It's dark outside now and the light from the fire and the oil lamps makes the berries glow while casting long looping shadows along the ceiling from the paper chains. The tree's lights are on too.

We have bangers and mash for dinner. Three fat ones each, turned chestnut brown in the skillet, and a pile of steaming mash. Its buttery smell covers my face and makes my mouth water as I lean over the plate.

'You any good at singing?' Jacob asks while we eat.

'Er, I wouldn't say good. I can hold a tune.'

'That'll do. How about a few carols? I thought I'd dust off that old thing.' He points to the antique organ that sits under the window on the far wall. It has a sort of concertina roller top and, under that, a keyboard that's smaller than a piano's, with yellowing ivory keys. Where the pedals would be on the piano there are two large foot pedals.

'You can play that?'

'Yes! It's an organ, a small one obviously. You push down on those pedals one at a time, a bit like a bike really, and that pumps air up through the pipes, and hey presto. Quite a bit smaller than the one I used to play in the church, but the same principle.'

He could have said many things, but I wouldn't have expected this. He's never once mentioned church before.

'I haven't played for quite a while, mind, but I'm sure it will come back. You up for it?'

'Definitely,' I say. 'I didn't realise you were religious.'

'Well, I'm not. But I do like church music, specially the organ stuff.'

'That's a turn-up for the books,' I say.

'Hidden depths,' he says, laughing and taking the plates over to the sink.

'I'll wash up,' I say.

'We can do that later. Let's see if I can find my hymn book.'

He goes over to the bookshelves and looks down towards the bottom, then pulls one out. 'Here we are. *Hymns Old and New*.'

He flips to the index at the back. The pages are the same wafer-thin paper that's in my little bible, and they rustle like dry leaves as he turns them.

'Yes,' he says, 'they're all here.' He scans through the index, calling out titles as he sees them.

'"Hark! the herald angels sing", "Once in royal David's city", "Good King Wenceslas", "In the bleak midwinter", "O come, all ye faithful", "The first Noel". What do you fancy?'

'I like "Hark! the herald",' I say.

'So do I. Let's start with that then.' Then he stops and looks up at me from the seat he's taken at the organ. 'Are you sure you're up to this? Feelin' all right? I don't want to give you a headache.'

'I'm fine,' I say. 'Definitely up for it.'

'All right then. Now, hang on.' He takes a box of matches

and lights two candles in the ornate brass holders on swinging arms either side of the music stand. They squeak a little as he moves them to bring the candlelight closer to the music.

'You'll have to stand over my shoulder to see the words.'

I can hardly see the music at all in this light, but it doesn't matter. The words of these carols are as embossed on my mind as the words of the Hail Mary and the Our Father.

'Right, let's see.' He begins pedalling, and a muffled hissing sound comes from somewhere inside the organ.

'That's the air going in,' Jacob says. 'Won't be a moment.'

He does a few more pedals with each foot then tests a key. A clear note sings out from somewhere at the back of the organ.

'Still working then,' Jacob says. 'Ready?'

'Ready,' I say.

He plays the introduction and we start singing. I've never heard Jacob sing before and I can't believe his voice. It's like he's from some Welsh men's choir. It's very powerful with a really nice, rich tone. It makes me more confident in my own not-as-good singing, so I belt it out too.

'You're really good,' I say when we're finished, 'Were you in a choir or something?'

'Not really,' he says, 'although I did sing with the lifeboatmen's choir when they were short, but that was a long time ago. Always enjoyed it, though. It's good for the soul.'

'Yeah, you're right,' I say and although I don't get the same tingle down my spine that I used to get with music, I do enjoy it. We do 'O come, all ye faithful', 'The first Noel', and then 'In the bleak midwinter'.

'That one's my favourite,' I say as we finish it and the final note of the organ fades in a faint sigh. 'Mum's too,' I add, thinking of how she loved crisp winter days and the nights closing in as the afternoons grew shorter.

'I miss your mum,' Jacob says.

'So do I.'

We're quiet for a minute, but it's not awkward, just a shared moment of peace.

'Almost nine o'clock,' Jacob says, standing and stretching his arms out.

'I'll do the washing up now,' I say.

'I'll wash, you dry,' Jacob says. It doesn't take long. I put everything away in the cupboards and then give the surface a wipe, neatly hanging the tea towel on the stove door handle. I like how clean and tidy this house is. There isn't too much stuff, and everything has its place. I get a feeling of being more in control of everything.

'Cup of tea before bed?'

'Yeah, go on then,' I say.

We sit in the armchairs by the fire with our tea, Jacob reading a book. I watch the glow in the wood burner, the surface of the embers rippling like a crimson sun glowing over the sea just before it sinks behind the horizon. My eyelids are drooping but I can't quite be bothered to get up out of the chair. Ridge sighs, shuffles and resettles on the floor.

'You need to be in bed,' Jacob says, looking up from his book, 'and for that matter, so do I.'

'Yes,' I say, standing and steadying myself as the usual dizziness surges and then passes. 'Night then.'

'Goodnight, Jago. I'll see you on Christmas morning.'

Ridge follows me up and jumps on to my bed, watching as I brush my teeth and splash water on my face. I hear the scrape of the wooden chair legs on the flagstones as Jacob pushes the chairs under the table, and then the shuck of the bolts on the door as he slides them across. Now, the rhythmic clump of his feet on the stairs. I blow out the oil lamp on my chest of drawers and strike a match to light my candle. Its light fills the room for an instant as the sulphur flares and dies back again. I change into my pyjamas, put on my dressing gown and sit by the window with the candle and my Gideon Bible. The little carving I've been doing for Jacob is finished now and it looks really nice with the candlelight casting tiny shadows in its dimpled surface. I flick through Luke's Gospel until I find the bit I'm looking for.

> *And in the same region there were shepherds out in the field, keeping watch over their flock by night. And an angel of the Lord appeared to them, and the glory of the Lord shone around them, and they were filled with great fear. And the angel said to them, 'Fear not, for behold, I bring you good news of great joy that will be for all the people. For unto you is born this day in the city of David a Saviour, who is Christ the Lord. And this will be a sign for you: you will find a baby wrapped in swaddling clothes and lying in a manger.' And suddenly there was with the angel a multitude of the heavenly host praising God and saying, 'Glory to God in the highest, and on earth peace among those with whom he is pleased.'*

The sky outside is clear now, the stars more brilliant than usual, their light chiselled sharp by the freezing air. I don't know if I believe in God or Jesus but I do believe in the story of Jesus, that he was real to people as a symbol of hope and goodness, because most people are good, I think, for all their faults and mistakes. People are attracted to goodness and look up to it, even if that's not how things always seem on the surface.

I think of the vision I had of the nurses in that Irish cottage hospital, huddled and talking quietly in the next room, their voices weaving together like an ancient music from somewhere deep in the earth. Maybe they were angels, but the feeling I had then was of a rebirth, of a mind free of worry and of all the marks and imprints of past experiences.

The same feeling comes to me now as the candle gutters in the faint draught coming through the windowpanes, and the snow outside shimmers like diamond dust, and the muffled squeak of Jacob's mattress springs drifts over the landing hall as he rolls over and settles again.

24

I wake up as my head jerks and it takes me a moment to get my bearings. My neck is stiff and the candle has burnt half the way down. I had fallen asleep propped up against the window. I need to get into bed. I blow out the candle and close my eyes as the afterglow of its coloured orb fades in my vision.

When I open my eyes again and look outside the window, the snow is even brighter in the moonlight now that the candle is out. I'm just about to stand to get into bed when I see a movement. Someone is walking down the lane towards the gate to the field. My heart quickens slightly. It's Sligo. It must be. This is it. If I don't follow him now I might never get the chance again.

I stroke Ridge and tell him to stay still and be quiet. I creep out of my room and pull the door softly behind me. Before I know it I'm downstairs, putting on my boots and very carefully sliding the bolts of the front door. In my backpack I have my torch and Jacob's camera.

Outside, the frozen crust over the snow crunches under my feet as I walk quickly towards the lane. I hear the horses stirring as I pass. I was expecting it to be heavy going walking through the snow, but it flies up in powdery blooms around my feet. Soon I'm at the top of the lane. I look up the hill to

Granny Carne's cottage and see a light on. Maybe she's seen him too. For a moment I'm paralysed with indecision. I swore I would stay away from Sligo. I could run up to her cottage and tell her this is our chance to get him. But by the time I get there and back it might be too late. I must decide what to do and the only way to do that is to act and not think. I head down the lane and just hope Granny Carne will understand.

The moon cuts sharp shadows over the snow and I walk close to the hedgerow where I'm shrouded in near darkness. It's bright enough, though, to see the cleft of the trail where Sligo has walked. I pause for a second to listen. The silence hums in my ears. There's no sound at all of anyone else. I quicken my pace, straining my eyes into the darkness ahead to make sure I don't catch up with him. When I get to the gate of the field I slow down. My breath sounds so loud in the silence that I wonder whether he might hear it, but of course he won't.

At the entrance to the field there is a perfect half-crescent in the snow where the gate has been pushed open and left that way. *Any idiot knows you close gates behind you in the country*, I think to myself, and then laugh slightly at what a stupid thought that is to have in this moment.

There's no sign of Bill Sligo in what I can see of the field ahead, but his track is clear: a dark vein of shadow running down the slope away from me. I look down at myself and can see my clothes quite clearly in the moonlight, like a dimly lit scene in a black-and-white film. I don't want to waste time but I don't want to be seen either, so instead of following his trail I hurry across the field towards the bushes at its edge, before going as quickly as I can down towards the mineshaft.

Then I hear it. Something about the still night and freezing air carries the heavy chunk of the diesel engine up from the water so clearly it could be a stone's throw away.

There he is, Sligo, same as last time, flashing his torch out to sea. The sound of the engine gets quieter now and I realise it's come in close, as the sound no longer travels straight up from the water, but has to make its way up the cliff and across to where I'm crouching in the protection of the shadows not more than a hundred feet from him. The engine cuts and the clink and rattle of Sligo opening the padlock rings out clearly followed by the sliding of the bolt. I can just make out his silhouette disappearing down the mineshaft.

After giving him a few moments to go down the shaft, I reach the opening myself, take the camera out of my bag, strap it around my neck, and wind the film on so it's ready to take a shot. Yesterday I changed it from the night setting that Jacob showed me to one for slightly better light assuming Sligo will have a torch down there. I just hope I've got this right.

It's inky black in the shaft as I lean over to look down but I think I can see a trace of light at the bottom, and I feel a bit dizzy with vertigo. I'm about to hoist myself up to the ledge when my oath to Granny Carne comes back to me again. *You're going to swear to me with Cadan Carne as a witness that you won't go near that man. All right?*

I shake my head at my promise to her. This could be the opportunity to get evidence of Sligo in the act of importing drugs. Then he'll be sent to prison where he should be already for what he did to Cadan Carne. Granny Carne will understand that, won't she? Anyway, I don't plan for Sligo to know I'm here – I'm going to go down and come back up without him realising.

I pull myself up, swing one leg over the ledge of the shaft, then the other, and grope around with my feet to feel the rungs of the ladder. My right foot catches on the first one. This is the tricky part now. I need to turn around so I'm facing the wall. I sort of roll over so my belly is on the freezing cold stone ledge, then I feel around again with my feet until they're both on the first rung. Very carefully I shift my weight on to the ladder and lower myself, holding on tight to the edge and stepping down until I can take the ladder in my hands.

Compared to the silvery light at the top, the shaft is like a black hole. I go slowly down, bit by bit, unable to see a thing. My breathing rasps noisily so I hold my breath and listen hard. I can hear voices now. As I start to climb down again, they get louder, and below me the disc of light at the bottom is getting bigger as I come closer to it. The voices are clear now. I hear Sligo's bark first.

'You're going to drop that in the water. Just throw them to me.' He sounds impatient. The reply is harder to hear. The man's speaking English but with a foreign accent.

I'm at the bottom now and I step gently off the ladder on to the stone floor. I have to duck down at first; then, after a couple of paces into the tunnel, I can stand, putting my hands up first to feel the height of the tunnel roof. It's only half a foot or so above my head. After the dark of the shaft, I can see quite clearly now. A white light that must be electric is casting shadows over the walls, picking out the roughly hewn rock on either side of me and above.

Ahead, maybe five metres, the tunnel goes to the left and disappears. Before that there's an opening, which must be to a side tunnel. I head towards it and slip into the darkness of its entrance. This is a perfect place to hide. I wonder whether it comes out somewhere else – perhaps there's another shaft – but I can't go looking now. Another time I'd like to, though.

Carefully, and very slowly, I take the lens cap off the camera. Edging my head out of the shadows I look towards the light, realising I'm going to have to go and look around the bend in the other tunnel if I want to see what Sligo is doing.

I edge out of the darkness and creep my way along the tunnel, being very careful not to scuff my feet on the ground. It must be deafening in here when the sea is up but tonight it's dead still and almost noiseless, just the occasional splash lapping the rocks beyond the tunnel entrance.

Sligo's voice rings out loud again and makes me start. 'How much more?' he asks sharply.

'Nearly finished,' comes the other reply.

This time the voice from outside the cave is clear, but deeper than the one I heard before. There must be two men in the boat, or maybe more. Noises are deceitful in this cave, their volume going up and down, making it hard to know how far away Sligo will be when I look around the corner. But I'd better look now or he'll finish and he might come back up the tunnel. Even with that side tunnel to hide in I will need to do it quickly. Plus I don't want to be stuck down here if Sligo locks the cover behind him as he leaves. I just need to take a photo and get out.

I peer round the bend with half of my face, and there he

is, not five metres away. He has his big broad back to me and he's taking packages the size of small bricks from one of the men in the boat, and stacking them along one wall of the cave.

I cast my eyes around the floor of the cave, looking to see if there's anything else. Two empty black holdalls lie on the ground not far from Sligo's feet. Should I take the shot now? No. I need to wait until he has the whole haul so the police can see how much there is. Also I can't see his face and there's not much use in a photo of his back; he'll just deny it's him.

'That's it, finished,' comes the voice from the boat. 'We're leaving.'

'Hold your horses.' Sligo's voice is raised and dangerous. 'I make that thirty-eight. It should be forty.'

'Yes, that's forty there,' comes the voice from the boat again.

'You wait. I'm counting them.'

At this, he turns around and I can see him clearly, the contours of his face chiselled by the sideways light of the electric lamp. I duck my head back into the shadows. This is it. This is the moment.

I just need to poke the camera round the corner and hold it firm against the rock so it doesn't blur when the shutter opens, like Jacob showed me. I just hope I've got the settings right. I'm ready now.

Slowly, I poke my head around again, this time holding the viewfinder of the camera to my eye, and very, very slowly, I squeeze my finger down on to the button.

25

The sound of the camera's shutter ricochets around the cave as if it's suddenly swarming with bats taking flight. Before I can even process how stupid I've been not to realise this would happen, Sligo looks up, straight at me, and I freeze.

For what seems like a very long time, neither of us moves or speaks.

'You,' he says at last, his face twisted with menace.

'What is it?' one of the men from the boat calls out urgently. Sligo ignores them, and takes a step towards me. Suddenly the roar of the boat's engine fills the cave and Sligo turns back towards the sea.

'Get back here!' he shouts. But the engine noise is now at a high pitch as the throttle opens and the boat pulls away from the cave.

Sligo stands there raging at the sea like a madman and for the first time I feel the danger of what I've done, and fear prickles through me. I turn and run, the way ahead very dark now with the light behind me. I run blindly forwards, hitting my arm on the stone wall as I go. Pain shoots down it, but I don't stop.

I hear Sligo's breath before I feel him, fast and heavy animal breathing. He grabs my coat and yanks me backwards.

I smell him now too. Damp clothes, acrid sweat and stale cigarette smoke.

He pushes me hard up against the wall and my head jerks back and smacks the rock. Straight away my head hurts inside and out, a searing pain shooting through it.

'Who's with you?' he shouts, his face so close to mine I can feel the heat of his breath.

'No one,' I say.

'Liar. Your uncle's up top, isn't he? That meddling bastard.'

'No, I swear, no one's here.'

Why did I say that? Why didn't I say Jacob was with me or at least had gone to the police, anything other than letting Sligo know I'm alone?

He turns his face towards the shaft and shouts, 'Jacob Trevarno!' Then he listens. The echo of his call peters out, leaving a thick silence all around us.

'You call him.'

I hesitate.

'Do it!' He shoves me again.

'Jacob!' I shout, dread filling me.

He looks back at me now, a grim smirk spreading across his face.

'So no one knows you're here,' he says softly. 'You thought you'd get one over on me, didn't you?'

He shoves me towards the cave opening, towards the sea.

'I could throw you in, let you drown or die of hypothermia,' he says.

He stoops down, still holding me tight, sweeps the floor with his free hand, and then finds what he's looking for. The cold echoing scrape of metal rings around the tunnel, and he lifts the pole up to show me, smiling with his mouth while his eyes stare at me emotionless like a shark.

My mind goes back to the coma, to the comfort of it, the safety of it, and I think to myself, *I died and came back to life for this?*

He pushes me hard, towards the cave entrance, and raises the metal pole above his head to bring it down on to mine, but I stumble backwards. He follows me towards the end of the tunnel and the drop down to the sea. I reach out and claw desperately at the wall, just managing to catch hold of the edge of a rock. Every muscle in my body tenses as I cling to it; but then I lose my balance and I fall.

'Get up.' His voice jolts me back, rough and harsh.

Sligo kicks me in the side and pain shoots through me like electricity.

'Get up, I said.' He shouts it, the anger over those men cheating him and me finding him smelting together. My side aches as I start to push myself up, trying to think at the same time. My mind is blank, but an instinct from somewhere flickers in me, and my own anger rises. Anger at him, at how he thinks he can push Jacob around; anger for Jacob who I don't think even knows how to be angry; anger at everything that happened: how I have to concentrate on every single thing I do, the mistakes I'm always making, the things I forget, the things I can't see, how I can't feel joy or excitement, how I'm so tired all the time. *All the time.*

I must focus. I just have to *do*, not think. If I stay close to Sligo, he won't be able to use that pole. Slowly I start to get up, staying slightly hunched over. I look upwards, just enough to see his body, but not his face. Then I rush at him, grabbing him around the waist. There's nothing in my mind but a burning rage that's spreading through my muscles and giving me the power to shove him up against the wall. I throw punches at him wildly, thrashing my fists from side to side, but he hardly moves, just grunts.

What now? I've got to run as fast as I can, and get to the ladder and up and out and away from this, away from him. I'm ready. I'm about to let go of him when my head wrenches back.

I can't work out what's happening, but then I feel the pain in my scalp where he's tugging hard at a handful of my hair. And now he's pushing me back and hitting me, and the fire that was in me has gone out. I can't stop him now. He's going to kill me: I know he is. I don't fear it. I already know death is painless. And I'm glad that I fought back, that I didn't just take it. But he's got me now and that's the way it is.

He pushes me hard and I stumble back towards the mouth of the tunnel. The light is behind him now, his black silhouetted arm rising up with the pole in his hand. It's very quiet, peaceful. Is he moving slowly or has time slowed down?

I'm aware of the pain in my body, but I don't feel it. I'm thinking about the nurses from my coma dream. Their soft lyrical murmuring, how mermaids would sing. I can hear the gentle splash of baby waves on the rocks below. I close my eyes and wait for the blow.

26

'You get away from him.'

The voice is loud and clear and powerful. When I open my eyes again Bill Sligo's dreadful silhouette is still there, but he's turning now, back towards the shaft.

He speaks, spitting out his words. 'You old bitch.'

All I can make out is the glare of his light as he takes a step away from me.

'Bill Sligo.' There's no mistaking the voice even though I can't see who it's coming from. It's Granny Carne.

'You can't help yourself, you interfering old bitch.'

'No,' she says, her voice very calm. 'You can't help *your*self, Bill Sligo. Greed, greed and violence. It's your mother's fault for never lovin' you.'

'You shut up.' There's something else in his voice, just a flicker of something, a sort of bitterness.

'No,' Granny Carne says. 'You be quiet. And get away from that boy.'

'Or what?' he asks, sneering. 'You're stupid for coming here, you old bitch. I'll finish you both.' He will too. Granny Carne is strong, very strong, but what's she going to do if he brings that pipe down on her head?

He moves away from me now and towards Granny Carne's voice. I still can't see her. I don't think he can either, because when he takes another step forward it is a cautious one. Before he can move again, she appears like a ghost out of the shadows.

Her face is almost white in this light, and it is transformed. Her usual warm smile has gone, her jaw is set, her lips thin and straight. Her twinkling eyes now stare coldly at him. She doesn't even glance at me.

He takes a step backwards now. Is he going to grab me? I shuffle my feet back, glancing down to see how close I am to the mouth of the cave. Very close. I put a hand out on to the cold damp stone to steady myself.

When I look up again my eyes catch something else that I couldn't see when I was looking straight at Granny Carne's face. She's holding something, something long and straight, the electric lamplight glancing off it. I can almost feel my brain flicking through options of what it might be. And then I realise. It's a shotgun. She's carrying her shotgun.

'Come here, Jago,' she says, still not taking her eyes off Sligo. I make to go past him, but he grabs me roughly and I stop. His grip is tight on my arm.

'Let him go, Sligo,' she says.

'No chance. Go on, take a shot. You'll kill us both, you old fool.'

'Not at this range,' she says.

'We both know that's bollocks. He'll be dead and in that sea and you'll have done it.'

She doesn't say anything to this, but she doesn't do anything either, which makes me think that what he said is right.

He keeps on talking. 'As it is, you're going to watch me choke the breath out of this one, then I'll deal with you.'

With this, he lifts the pole in the hand he's not holding me with, and puts it across my throat. It's ice cold.

Granny Carne steps forward.

'Not another inch,' Sligo says. His voice is quick now. I feel his breath on my neck, and it smells of stale tobacco and decay. The bar is clamping down on me and making it hard to breathe, and as I struggle against it the most intense feeling rises up in me. *No, you're not going to kill me. I'm not having it.* I know what to do now. And without thinking, without me deciding to do it, it just happens.

Very fast, I lift up my right arm and my body surges with strength as if every bit of energy that I've been missing for all these months has been stored up in me for this moment. Then I bring my elbow down with my full force and swing it back into his stomach. He goes down straight away. He lets go of me but grabs my ankle as I run, an animal grunt coming from him. I roll over and shuffle myself away from him. He still has my ankle. I lift my other leg and boot him hard in the shoulder. He lets go of me and half stands. He's still very winded. I scramble back, roll over on to my knees and lurch towards Granny Carne, struggling to catch my own breath.

The noise rings out before I can even look around: an almighty bang that makes everything in me vibrate, like a bell being struck by a hammer. Then another. I turn my head to see Sligo staggering backwards. All the twisted menace has been stripped from his face, leaving a look of total surprise.

His feet are at the edge of the tunnel entrance. He puts his arms out as if to catch himself, but there's no conviction in the movement. It's nothing more than a flailing impulse. His hands brush the rocks either side of him; he topples back with his mouth gaping open like a fish and then he disappears. A heartbeat later, a splash sounds around us, followed by silence as the ringing in my ears recedes.

I step forwards, meaning to look over the edge, but Granny Carne calls to me.

'Wait,' she says, 'let me look.'

She picks up the electric lamp and goes past me, holding it out over the water below. Coming to stand next to her, I look down too, and there he is, floating face down, his body bobbing in the swell. Those men in the boat are well away. There's not a sound coming from out to sea.

'There,' Granny Carne says. 'He's gone.'

'Yes,' I say, and neither of us speaks for a while.

The pain in my side comes back now and I pull up my top to have a look. There's no blood and when I push carefully on my ribs they hurt but they don't feel broken.

'You all right, Jago?' she asks.

'Oh yeah, I'm all right,' I say.

'All right then. Let's go.'

'What about all this?' I say, pointing at the packets now scattered over the floor of the cave. They're exactly like the ones I've seen on those drug-raid TV programmes. Tight brick-sized packages, mustard-brown inside.

'I think it's heroin,' I say. 'Those men might come back for it.'

'I very much doubt that. They got their money. Do you have a knife?' she asks.

I'd forgotten about that. All along I had my penknife in my pocket. I take it out now.

'Right,' she says, 'slash those and chuck 'em in the sea.'

I do as she says, stabbing my knife into the packages, ripping them open and throwing them into the water.

'All of this must be worth thousands of pounds,' I say as I rip open another package. It's taking some time as there are so many.

'More than that, I shouldn't wonder.'

After a while, she asks, 'Is that it? All done?'

'Yeah.'

'Come on then.' She picks up the lantern and has another look around.

'We'll leave that,' she says, nodding at the empty holdall.

I pause and look at her. 'Will you be all right on the ladder?' I ask. She just looks at me and sets off, and I remember watching her shimmying up and down the ladder in front of her cottage to clean out the gutters.

As we go up, the musty smell of the deeper part of the shaft is replaced by a slight breeze coming down, and the circle of light at the top grows larger. We're both out of breath when, minutes later, we land ourselves on the snow by the shaft opening.

'We better close that,' Granny Carne says, looking at the cover for the shaft. 'And lock it.'

I do it, and the slamming of the wood makes me jump as I drop it down into place.

'Give me the key,' she says.

I pass it to her and she walks a few steps towards the cliff and throws it into the sea.

'Come on,' she says, and she puts her arm through mine as we start to walk home.

27

'What a beautiful night,' Granny Carne says, her face shining in the moonlight as she gazes up at the sky. She looks very alive, exhilarated. It seems a strange thing for her to say, but she's right, it is. Above us, millions of stars twinkle bright against the night sky.

'One of those might be the star of Bethlehem,' she says. 'Happy Christmas, by the way.'

'Oh yeah,' I say. 'Happy Christmas. Is it real, the star of Bethlehem?'

'In truth, I don't know,' she says, and we walk quietly after that, the only sound being the crunching of our steps in the snow.

When we're almost at the farm, I stop.

'Before we go in,' I say, 'I know I broke my oath to you and I'm really sorry. I didn't want to. But after Sligo set fire to the barn, it was like he was closing in and I knew he wasn't going to stop, so I had to do something.'

Then something occurs to me. I don't why I haven't already thought it. How did she know I was there? And then I remember what Jacob had told me, her second sight.

'You knew I'd broken the oath tonight, didn't you? That's why you came after me.'

She puts her arm through mine and pulls me close.

'None of that matters now,' she says, and I know she's not going to say anything more.

'Jacob's up,' I say, looking at the little square window glowing butter-yellow from the lamplight within.

'I'd better come in with you,' Granny Carne says when we get to the gate. 'That dog's woken him.'

I can hear Ridge's muffled bark through the door as we approach. When I squeeze the latch and open the door, he jumps at me, but the thing I see is Jacob standing right behind him putting on his coat.

'Jago!' he says. 'Where have you been? I was just about to come out looking for you.'

I see how worried he looks. His face is creased and seems somehow older.

'Sorry,' I say, 'I didn't mean to wake you.'

'You didn't. This lunatic just started barking his head off a few minutes ago, sprinting between your door and the front door. Well, I looked into your room and you weren't there. What's happened?'

Then: 'Morvoren!' he says, seeing her behind me in the darkness. 'What's going on? Are you both all right?'

'Well, move out of the door, let us in, and I'll tell you,' she says. 'And yes, he's fine, I'm fine, so stop your worrying and shift it.' She ushers me forwards, into the warmth of the farmhouse.

It's a huge relief to be back inside, the last embers of the fire glowing and two oil lamps burning. I suddenly feel exhausted, and I sit back heavily into the armchair. The kettle clunks as Jacob puts it on to the stovetop. Granny Carne sits down too.

'Well?' Jacob asks, coming over to us. He doesn't sound angry. Sort of confused and a bit startled from being woken up.

'The long and short of it,' Granny Carne says, 'is that that brute Bill Sligo is dead.' She says it as if she's commenting on the weather, and it calms me.

Jacob is speechless for a bit.

'What?' he says once he's gathered himself. 'What do you mean?'

And then we get into it, me and Granny Carne, the whole thing, everything that's happened. I try to tell them every detail of what's led up to tonight, but I keep forgetting things, and having to go back. But I think he gets the gist of it pretty clearly. He doesn't say anything the whole time we are talking, which is for quite a while as I go over all the bits about how I worked out what Bill Sligo was up to and why he wanted Jacob's field so much.

'So you see,' Granny Carne says once we're finished. 'Jago actually had nothing to do with killing Sligo. It was all me.'

'Apart from creeping out and almost getting killed by that nutter,' Jacob says.

'Apart from that,' Granny says, her face unreadable.

'Hang on,' Jacob says to Granny Carne. 'How did you know Jago was there?'

I look at her and I know she won't tell him about the oath.

'I was closing my curtains for bed when I saw Sligo sloping down the lane, and heading towards your farm, Jacob. Knowing what Jago had told me, I followed him. Well, I've been watchin' and followin' him for years, waitin' for him to slip up. He was faster than me and I got to the field just in time to see Jago going down that mineshaft.'

'Well, thank God you did,' Jacob says. 'And what about the shaft now?'

'Locked up. We threw away the key, and I suggest you leave it like that.'

'And when Sligo's body washes up?'

'What about it?' she says. 'Everyone from Land's End to Camborne knows he's rotten to the core. Was rotten to the core, I should say. No one will be surprised someone finally finished him off. And I'll tell you one thing, Jacob Trevarno, there's not a person alive would think he was killed by the mad old witch who lives up on the hill. Imagine!' She laughs at this, and even Jacob's face softens, but not quite to a smile. 'Jago, neither,' she says. 'What business has he got with Bill Sligo? None.'

'No, I suppose that's right,' Jacob says. 'Yes,' he adds, the thought sinking in, 'yes, I think you might be right about that. What a thing to die for, though, a scraggly little field that's good for nothing but a bit of pasture. Pass me that camera, Jago.' He opens it, takes out the film and throws it into the stove.

'There,' Jacob says. 'That's that then. And what about you, Jago? Are you all right?'

'I'm fine,' I say, and I am.

'It's the adrenaline,' Jacob says. 'Sounds like you took a right beating. Let's have a look at you.' He pulls my jumper up to reveal big red welts along my ribs. He whistles through his teeth and says 'Bastard' under his breath.

'Yes, well, the boy's all right and no one's going to be

doing that to him again. You need a bit of witch hazel on that,' Granny Carne says.

'I think I've got some actually,' Jacob says, and he goes upstairs to get it.

'Thanks, Granny Carne, for everything,' I say.

'Nothing to thank me for. I've been waiting for that moment for a very long time.'

If anyone else had said something like that, I think I'd have been shocked, but I understand what she means. It's like a worldly justice has happened, something inevitable.

Suddenly I'm overcome with tiredness and every bit of me is aching for sleep.

'I've got to go up.'

'Yes, you go up,' Jacob says, coming down the stairs and handing me the tube of witch hazel. 'And make sure you sleep in.'

'I will.'

'And I'll be going too,' Granny Carne says.

'I'll walk you back,' Jacob says.

'You will not.'

'Fine, but join us for lunch tomorrow, will you?' Jacob asks her.

'All right then, I will.'

'One o'clock,' he says.

'Night,' I say from the stairs.

I'm too tired to undress. I lie on the bed, pull over a blanket and fall straight to sleep.

28

It's late when I wake, just past eleven. I feel better for the sleep, but still sick with tiredness and I have a sharp headache. Downstairs, Jacob is busy in the kitchen, but I can only just hear the muffled clink of dishes and pots and pans. He's obviously trying to be quiet. I want to get up and see him. I have a quick wash in the sink and put on a clean shirt and jumper. The smells coming up the stairs when I open my door make my stomach rumble.

'Merry Christmas!' I say as I get to the bottom of the stairs.

'Merry Christmas, Jago!' he says, coming over and giving me a hug.

'You on it already?' I say, looking over at the glass of port on the side by where he's cooking.

'Oh, just a drop to help me along.'

'Smells really good,' I say.

'Hope so. That goose is a real beaut of a bird. So much meat on it, we'll be the stuffed ones.'

'Great.'

'How you feeling after last night?'

'What, like tired? Or . . .' I trail off.

'Well, you know, everything.'

I think for a little bit.

'Well, fine actually, I think. I mean, obviously it wasn't nice, the whole thing . . . but, well, he brought it on himself, didn't he? I mean, I only went down to the field because I knew he was up to something on your land and had been really threatening. And Granny Carne only followed me down there because she thought I was in danger, and she was right. And she only did what she did because, well . . .' I trail off again.

'Because he was gonna kill the pair of you.'

'Well, yeah, so it's like he started a train of events that led to what happened, and it was him what made things get worse and worse. So, you know, in a way he sort of made it happen.'

'Hmm.' Jacob pauses before saying, 'That's very philosophical of you, Jago.'

I feel worried now. 'You don't agree?'

He seems surprised. 'Absolutely I do,' he says firmly. 'Absolutely. That man was going to come to an end like that one way or another, no doubt about it, I just wouldn't have thought for a million years it would've involved you and Morvoren Carne.'

'No,' I say. 'I'm also glad that he won't be hassling us any more and maybe Granny Carne can feel a bit more peaceful about Cadan now. That'd be good.'

'You're a very kind lad, Jago. It's a good quality in a person.'

'So are you,' I say, a bit embarrassed.

'Well,' Jacob says, rolling a colander of potatoes into the sink, 'I shouldn't wonder if Morvoren doesn't even mention last night when she's here later. She's not one for talking things over. She's a *what's done is done* kind of person, 'cept with Cadan of course. I don't suppose there will ever be a proper end to that for her, even after last night. So maybe we'll be guided by her on that, all right? You were there too, but she's the one what done it, so it's her business anyway really.'

'All right,' I say, relieved at the idea of not having to go over it all again.

'Not that we shouldn't talk about it if you want to, like. We should, if that's the case, I mean. It's not good to bottle things up, is it?'

'It's fine,' I say, 'but thank you.'

'All right. Well, if you ever do, then go ahead, that's all I'm saying. I'm happy to talk about anything with you.'

'Thank you.'

'Right then, I'd better get on with this food, hadn't I?' he says.

'What can I do?'

'Well, start by making a nice coffee, will you? Oh, and I almost forgot,' he says, 'I got your Christmas present.'

'I got you one too,' I say.

'Well, aren't we the lucky ones?'

'I'll just go and get yours,' I say and I head back upstairs.

'I made it,' I say, handing over the carved horse.

'That's Niamh!' he says, holding it at arm's length and turning it in his hand to look at it from all sides. 'That's great, really great. Thank you. You know, you could sell this sort of thing down the farmers' market, or that craft fair in the Guildhall. People would love them.'

'Maybe,' I say.

'Here's yours.' He holds out something wrapped in bright red tissue paper. It's a pocket guidebook to the wild birds of Cornwall. A beautiful edition, second-hand and in great condition, the ivy-green hardback cover only very slightly faded, embossed with gold lettering. Inside, the pages are a lovely thick paper, faded sepia-coloured and spotted with age. I open it and the sweet smell of antique bric-a-brac shops wafts up from the pages. There are line drawings of the birds and their feathers and descriptions of each one's main features underneath.

'It's perfect. Where did you get it?'

'Book sale in St Just.'

'I really like it,' I say. 'Thank you.'

'You're welcome. Oh, and this came for you day before yesterday. I put it aside as I thought it was probably a present.'

I open the parcel and the wrapping paper and inside is a mobile phone. There's a card too.

'Who's that from?' Jacob asks.

'Sophie,' I say. 'She says if Jacob won't put in a phone like a normal person, I'll need this.'

'The cheek!' Jacob says, laughing.

'Can I plug it in by the outside freezer?'

'Of course you can. Then do you fancy peelin' a few potatoes once you've done that?'

It's coming up for midday when I finish the potatoes and help get the rest of the veg ready. Sprouts, which I hate, and some kale.

'I'll just get these spuds into the oven, then that's it apart from the gravy, but I need the veg water for that.'

'Anything else I can do?' I ask.

'You could lay the table if that's all right. There's the fancy stuff in that cupboard.' He nods at the very old, dark-chocolate-coloured wooden cupboard that I don't think I've ever actually opened. 'Should be some nice glasses, cutlery and plates in there. Some proper napkins too, I think.'

'Yep, I've got them,' I say, looking into the dark space inside.

The glasses are those chunky cut-crystal ones and the cutlery is silver with bone handles.

'Granny Carne won't believe it,' I say.

'Hidden depths, Jago,' Jacob says.

'It's nice,' I say, laying three places.

'Your grandmother's stuff, that is.'

'Bloody hell,' I say, putting one of the crystal glasses back into the cupboard. 'I'll just have a normal one, I think.'

He laughs. 'As you wish.'

The kitchen is steamy and filled with smells that are making my mouth water. Roasted goose and roast potatoes and the gravy bubbling on the stove. It's warm and the fire is crackling and occasionally hissing. I'm sleepy again already but in a nice way this time. Like being wrapped up in blankets.

'A little toast,' Jacob says, raising his port glass, 'before she arrives.'

'All right.' I lift my glass of cloudy apple juice.

'Obviously the circumstances that brought you here weren't the best,' Jacob says, 'and I'm not saying I'm glad it happened or anything like that, but I am glad you're here. I would say I'm proud of you, how you faced all this, but I have no business being proud of you. You're not my achievement. But you should be proud of yourself. And whatever happens now I'm just glad we've had this time together.'

'Me too. I love being here with you,' I say, looking down. 'You know I'm not about to die, though, don't you?'

'I should bloody hope not. I'm counting on you to eat most of that goose. Speaking of which, let's have a look at her.'

He opens the stove door and steam billows out the way clouds bloom in a blue sky.

'Looks all right, don't you think?'

'Really good,' I say, looking at the skin crisped to a dark shade of amber.

'Reckon we can let her rest now.' He lifts the roasting tray out and covers the goose with foil and a blanket of tea towels.

'Just the potatoes to finish off and the veg and that's it. Oh, and I must add some of that veg water to the gravy. Time for a little Christmas drink, I think,' he says pouring another port.

'How many of those have you had?'

'Two little thimbles thus far, officer, with the intention of more.'

I laugh at this. I'm glad he's having a good time.

'Come on then,' he says, sitting down, 'let's have a bit of quiet time before Morvoren gets here.'

29

The knocker makes me start.

'That'll be her,' Jacob says. 'Will you let her in?'

Granny Carne takes both my hands in hers when I open the door and gives them a shake.

'Bit peaky,' she says, looking at me with her appraising eye. 'Tired, I should think. Did you sleep?'

'Yeah, I did, for ages.'

'Good boy. Let's see what old Jacob's been up to in that kitchen then,' she says, stepping inside.

'Smells good! And look at all this,' she says, taking in the room. 'I didn't know you had it in you, Jacob Trevarno.'

'Well, we've an important guest today, see. Here,' he says, holding out a glass of port to her. 'Good health.'

'Well, I won't say I can't believe it, as that would be rude,' Granny Carne says, wiping her mouth with her napkin. 'But that was a triumph, Jacob.'

'Well, thank you, I think,' Jacob says, laughing.

'It was great!' I say, and it was. The goose had the crispiest skin and juicy dark meat. The potatoes had thick golden crusts with fluffy insides. The veg I wasn't so bothered about, but Granny Carne wouldn't let me get away with having none.

'Greens!' she said, jabbing her fork at my plate.

Already it's getting dark outside, the dusk giving way to night so that when Jacob pours brandy over the Christmas pudding and lights it, the blue rolling flames light up our faces and then crackle before petering out.

'This is nice,' Jacob says, 'us together on Christmas Day, and after everything.'

The light of the oil lamps falls on Jacob's face. He looks very peaceful, full of food and wine.

'After all, it might be the only year you're here,' he carries on.

Suddenly I am alert. Does he want me to move on? Find my own way again? I can't even imagine it. I like living here, I like being with Jacob, and I really don't know how well I'd manage on my own.

'Nonsense,' Granny Carne says, 'Jago's stopping here, ain't that right, Jago?' And she puts her warm hand on mine.

'Are you?' Jacob asks. His eyes and voice seem to brighten. Perhaps he wants me to stay? And then I think if I've learned anything this year it's don't waste time doing things you don't want to do, or not saying things that should be said.

'Would that be all right?' I ask, looking down at my empty bowl.

'All right? Of course it's all right. I'd be lying if I said I hadn't been hoping you would stay, but I didn't want to assume anything, like. This is your home for as long as you want it to be, Jago. But you know you're young still, with a lot of years ahead of you, a lot of things you'll want to do when you're ready. You've got to make the decisions you need to make without thinking about me, all right?'

'All right,' I say.

'Well, then,' Granny Carne says. 'Good.'

30

It's proper dark by the time Granny Carne leaves. We both want to walk her home but she won't have it so we sit for a while, drinking tea and watching the fire die down until my eyelids are heavy with sleep.

'I'm turning in,' I say. 'Thanks for a great Christmas, Jacob, it was the best, really.'

'Thank you, Jago. We had a good time, I think, don't you?'

'Yeah, I do. Right then, night.'

'Goodnight, Jago.'

Up in bed, I'm floating in that liminal space before sleep, wrapped in a shroud of total calm. I can't feel my body; I'm not thinking. Far away I hear bleeping, slow and regular, bleep bleep bleep, like whales singing to each other fathoms below the sea, and the mechanical waves like an accordion that lost its voice, whoosh click whoosh click.

And there, just through the doorway, in glowing yellow light, people are sitting around a table, murmuring to each other, their voices a soft pulsing song like the heartbeat of the earth.

I have given myself to them and their happiness radiates out of them and into me. I float in the soothing waves of their lilting song. Perhaps the light is coming from them. Perhaps they are angels.

Acknowledgements

Thank you to everyone involved in saving my life when I had a cardiac arrest in 2021. Special thanks to my wife and children who raised the alarm; my friend Peter, who gave me CPR; and the paramedics of the London Ambulance Service, who persisted in trying to restart my heart and ultimately succeeded. Without those people, I would not be here today.

Thank you to my sister, Tess, and my brother-in-law, Freddie, who helped my family so much when I was in hospital and have supported us ever since.

I have received and continue to receive truly excellent care from so many doctors, nurses and other health professionals. I am grateful to everyone who has looked after me and who still looks after me. Their kindness and expertise have made an enormous difference, helping me learn how to live my new life.

There came a point during the fourth year after the cardiac arrest that I started to look for a new purpose, having not been able to return to work. I had been slowly writing this novel, and I decided to send it out. I would like to thank Caradoc King, Amy Mitchell and Rebecca Percival at United Agents for their expertise and encouragement and for giving the novel such a good start.

ACKNOWLEDGEMENTS

I would also like to thank Selina Walker, my editor at Hutchinson Heinemann, who, as well as being a wonderful editor, has been thoughtful, kind and understanding. Thank you also to the whole team at Hutchinson Heinemann. I feel very fortunate to have so many talented and dedicated people working on my novel.

Finally, I would like to thank all of my family and my friends. You have all been so loving and supportive.

The character of Granny Carne in this novel first appeared in a 2005 young adult novel, *Ingo*, written by my late mother, Helen Dunmore, and published by HarperCollins. Granny Carne stayed with me and it seemed natural to include her in my novel, albeit in a slightly altered version of herself. It was also important to me to have a connection with my late mother's work.

For that same reason, Jago is named after Jago from *The Ferry Birds*, a children's picture book that my late mother and I worked on together, published by Mabecron Books in 2010.

The verse that Jago in this novel remembers – towards the end – is one of my late mother's poems, 'The Thorn', which appeared in her 1997 collection, *Bestiary* (Bloodaxe Books), although Jago misremembers the exact wording.

Bringing a book from manuscript to what you are reading is a team effort, and Penguin Random House would like to thank everyone at Hutchinson Heinemann who helped to publish *This, My Second Life*.

PUBLISHER
Selina Walker

EDITORIAL
Laurie Ip Fung Chun
Richenda Todd
Mary Karayel

DESIGN
Dan Simpkins

PRODUCTION
Nicky Nevin

INVENTORY
Lizzy Moyes

UK SALES
Alice Gomer
Emily Harvey
Kirsten Greenwood
Phoenix Curland

INTERNATIONAL SALES
Anna Curvis
Barbora Sabolova

PUBLICITY
Marie-Louise Patton

MARKETING
Lucas Lockyer

AUDIO
Meredith Benson
Elenya Havard Griffiths